# Holy Terror

Also by Steve Abbott:


*Wrecked Hearts.*  Dancing Rock Press, 1978.
*Lives of the Poets.*  Black Star Series, 1987.
*Skinny Trip to a Far Place.*  e.g. press, 1988.
*View Askew: Postmodern Investigations*
    (critical essays).  Androgyne Press, 1989.

# HOLY TERROR

## by Steve Abbott

The Crossing Press
Freedom, California 95019

**Library of Congress Cataloging-in-Publication Data**

Abbott, Steve,  1943-
     Holy terror.

     I.  Title.
PS3551.B267H65 1989    813' .54    89-17344
ISBN 0-89594-383-2
ISBN 0-89594-382-4 (pbk.)

The following work is a fiction based on dream journals. No reference to persons, places or events should be taken as factual. Phrases, parodies, and episodes condensed from earlier works echo throughout the text. Authors pastiched include Bataille, Broch, Hart Crane, Dante, DeSade, Dostoyevski, Genet, Pierre Klossowski, Matthew Lewis, John Marston, Rabelais, Robbe-Grillet, etc. (after several years and many rewrites, I've long since lost track of them all.)

S.A.

How sweet it is to live as one like brothers,
like precious ointment flowing down the beard,
down the beard of Aaron.

— Psalm 133

# The Monastery

# One

Scarcely had the basilica bell tolled five minutes and already the church was thronged. Don't assume that this crowd was assembled either from motives of piety or thirst for God. Scandal and curiosity brought them here. For an entirely different reason I would have been present myself, weeping and wailing, but I'd been locked in a cell. All I could do was thrash my fists against cold plaster. Back and forth I paced, eight steps from window to door. The only furniture: my cot, one wooden table, one chair.

Didn't some of these townspeople, seminarians and novices below love Robbie? Might not some, at least, be as innocent as I when I first came to Inviolate? Questions turned in my mind like embers as I stared out the heavy, oak-framed window, wishing I were a cloud, a bird, anything but what I was. How different I'd first felt upon my arrival at Inviolate Conception Abbey.

Nestled in a valley between three hills, Inviolate looked just like you'd expect a monastery to look only without any thick surrounding walls. It had two small lakes, one polluted and one not. Around its small cluster of buildings yawned acre after acre of rich Iowa loam. Brother monks managed the farms and print shop. Priest monks managed the seminary. God managed the rest — or so I thought.

Speeding down Highway 55 in Father John's black Cadillac, fields of corn, wheat, grazing land and sky blurred together like huge peaceful shapes on a Rothko canvas. Meditative shapes. And like the hypnotic white stripe painted down the center of highways one follows at night, they urged me to anticipate my destination with utmost eagerness.

We pulled into the parking lot about 12:30 p.m., my heart fluttering like Hail Marys at a novena. Young monks and seminarians were just leaving the dining hall. Clustered in groups of two and three, their black cassocks looked harsh in the afternoon sunlight. They moved slowly, a slight breeze billowing the hems of their garments.

Climbing the slope to the monastery entrance, we passed a small grotto. It must have taken someone years to fit so many tiny bits of stone and colored glass into the cement of the shrine. Peaceful work, devotional work, not alienated labor such as I'd suffered working in department stores with cranky bosses on my back. For some reason I didn't want anyone to see me and felt relieved when we got to the door.

Brother Luke was probably suited to no other task than that of doorkeeper. An elderly, one-eyed man with a limp and a lower lip paralyzed in to a scowl, he ushered us into a chilly waiting room. Father Adelheim was expecting us, he said. I looked at Father John. "One doesn't go to a monastery to escape," he'd lectured me on our drive from Milo. "There *is* no escape." He had a bloom on his cheeks. For myself, I found the paved parking lot and new cars in front of the monastery a disappointment. Brother Luke and the dank tranquility of the waiting room were more to my liking.

"Ahem . . ."

Father Adelheim had slipped into the room and stood looking at us, hands folded and with a benevolent smile.

"So you've brought us a new recruit."

He licked his lips and scratched at his potato nose.

While Adelheim and Father John exchanged pleasantries, I tried not to stare at Adelheim's stiff wig. Were all monks hairless? Would I too have to shave my head if

I stayed? I fixed my eyes on a tile mosaic of the monastic seal which was set into the center of the floor. A cracked cup with wings. There was an absence of dirt and cobwebs in the corners and a peculiar odor of stone in the room. I imagined the invention of a new deodorant: "Monastery Mist — the odor of holiness!" Suddenly I heard myself addressed.

"So you want to be a priest! I suppose you know Latin?"

Adelheim had sat down, his elbows resting on the brown leather arms of his chair. With his right thumb and forefinger he pulled at his chin and kneaded his lower lip as if they were made of dough.

"Not exactly, Father."

I looked back to the floor, filled with confusion. Although raised Catholic, I'd never attended Catholic school or felt integrated within the Church. Priests and nuns still made me uncomfortable. My sole aim in coming had been to get out of Milo. I couldn't stand being around vain, cynical intellectuals any longer but hanging out with department store clerks was still less appealing.

Trollson, a friend from college, had given me Thomas Merton's *Seven Storey Mountain* to read. It struck home. I too was sick of debauchery, aimlessness, empty pomposity, not to mention my general lack of identity. Besides, everyone I knew was leaving Milo for the summer except me. So I'd gone to Father John, the Catholic chaplain, to ask him if he knew of a monastery where I might work. Hadn't Wittgenstein spent two years in an Austrian monastery? But never in my wildest dreams had I entertained the idea of becoming a parish priest. Bake sales? Weddings? Forget it!

"You don't want to become a priest or you don't know Latin?"

Adelheim's face remained fixed in its benevolent wince. I was desperate. Having told everyone I was going to a monastery, the last thing I wanted was to return, a reject. Hadn't Father John already explained my intentions? Hadn't the monastic authorities approved?

"I'm not sure, Father. I wanted to see what it would be like living and working here first."

"Well, you'll need Latin in any event." Adelheim stood, his robe pouring forward like a river over his now vanished knees, "Our summer school program starts in a week, but let's look around before it gets late. I'll start by showing you your dorm."

I sighed with relief. Though I hated languages, I would have studied Swahili rather than return to Milo. After our tour, I watched Father John's Cadillac float off in a cloud of dust, its black tailfins like sails on a departing ship. I couldn't concentrate on Adelheim's words any more. The priest question still rattled me. Priest! Priest!

That night I dreamt I was celebrating Mass. The air grew increasingly thick with each metallic clank of the censor. My eyes stung. My arms ached under heavy, brocaded vestments as I raised a gold chalice high above my head.

"HOC EST ENIM . . . ."

The congregation, including Trollson, my mother, grandparents, everyone I'd ever known, grew deathly still.

"HOC EST ENIM . . . ."

My throat constricted and my tongue went dry. I couldn't remember the words and gestures for the Consecration.

Early the next morning the basilica bell began gonging, its slow reverberations a magnified heartbeat pulling me from sleep. Shivering, I donned black pants, shoes and a cassock Father Adelheim had given me the day before. Sharp, cold air filled my nostrils. I studied the shadowy wooden table and bed of my room, the plain white walls. Severe, yet protective, the bell kept gonging. It sounded alive. I felt like a child. I felt I had just stepped out of a time machine and into the Dark Ages. This pleased me.

Quickly I hastened from my room, sped to the end of the long hallway and down the polished oak stairway into the courtyard. Small electric lamps illumined hooded figures scurrying along a brick path. I followed in silence. Silence was the rule before breakfast and after dinner. Someone pointed me to a pew where I stood with a couple of other seminarians.

Such a vast and peaceful interior, arches duplicating ad infinitum like arms reaching up to heaven. Dim lights shone down on frescoes in the style of Fra Angelico. In the intersection of the cross-shaped basilica, a six foot wide disk hung down seventy feet from the ceiling. Beneath the disk stood a large marble slab, the altar, which was surrounded by irises and guelder-roses. Flowers, I thought, the sexual organs of plants. Here time did not move as in the outside world. Was this the rhythm of the Middle Ages? It pleased me.

For over thirteen hundred years, monks had been singing the hours of the day. Every five hours they flowed form the rear of the basilica double file, moving like a waterfall down the three steps toward the altar. Bowing first toward the altar, then to each other, they backed single file into facing choir stalls. Then, back and forth, psalm verse began alternating in a monotone stream of song:

*Intenday-vochi-orachiownis MAY-HE*
*Rex mayus et dayus MAY-US*
*Quoaneam-odd-teyorabo DOMI-NAY*
*Money ex owdyvochem MAY-HEM*

I shut my eyes. I couldn't understand the words but something deeper in me moved.

*Money-as-tabo-et VID-EO*
*Quoanem non dayo VO-LENS*
*Iniquitatem TU-EZ . . . .*

I felt myself starting to rise and grabbed the rough stained wooden pew in front of me. I didn't want to end up on the ceiling like some helium-filled balloon. Secure I was still on the floor, I again opened my eyes. The altar was now illumined by four spotlights and glowed eerily.

Then, from deepest silence, a pipe organ erupted from subterranean bass to shriek into highest tremolo. The run tore my mind like a piece of paper. It filled the basilica till the walls vibrated. A priest in flowing green chasuble moved toward the altar flanked by two acolytes in stark white surplices. His gestures were wide and broad. When he spoke, his voice echoed.

"DOMINUS VOBISCUM!"

He sounded magnificent, powerful, not pinched and dry like the parish priests of my youth.

After Mass I was free to wander outside. A glow of magenta filled the eastern sky as I sat on the bluff overlooking the baseball field. Gradually daubs of yellow and gold spilled over onto the purple-green loam of the distant hills. How clean the air smelled. From under the low stone wall where I sat, a small bush pushed out new leaves each day, unfolding and reaching toward the sun. How many monks had sat where I sat now watching nature celebrate its own Mass?

For the first few weeks I was content to savor this simplicity. Never had I felt so happy. I'd read a few pages of Thomas a Kempis, eat breakfast in silence according to the Rule, and go to the library rare book room. Although I'd originally hoped for a more penitential, manual labor, making art slides was quiet and pleasant.

Carefully I'd cut squares of film from the roll, set them between two thin pieces of glass, press them into metal frames and label them. Then I'd hold each slide up to the window to make sure they were properly centered.

Outside was a maple tree in which a robin would often perch and sing. Sometimes two old monks, Raymond and Willibald, would come in to coat the old leather books with oil to keep them from cracking. Like birds, they chattered constantly. Raymond was small, thin and serious. Willibald was tall, portly and mischievous.

When he learned I was an artist, Raymond wanted to show me an illustration he'd once done using the old egg tempera technique. "There's the cow," he squeaked in his reedy voice, "and there's the Virgin . . . and there's . . . ."

"And there's the monkey," Willibald interrupted.

Raymond squinted at the page intently. "That's no monkey," he straightened up and scolded. "That's a *wiseman.*"

"No it's not," Willibald persisted. "It's a monkey see? Look at those ears." Raymond peered down again, utterly bewildered, till Willibald's cascade of laughter made him look up. Then he shook his fist and stomped out threatening to tell the abbot Willibald had blasphemed.

"I didn't say it *was* a monkey," Willibald protested. "I only said how you painted the ears made it *look* like one."

Raymond was one of the last of the original monks form Switzerland and the ways of contemporary youth scandalized him. Once I was talking to him in the grotto above the parking lot when two seminarians in gym shorts ran by toward the handball court. Raymond turned and covered his eyes. "Ach!" he exclaimed, "I took a vow of chastity."

When not working in the rare book room I paged through theological magazines or shelved books. Sometimes I had time to peruse books others had checked out. I learned Catholicism was not simply the one-dimensional dogma I'd been taught in parish sermons and catechism classes. Monasticism itself was an old, complex tradition.

St. Benedict, like many well born young men in 500 A.D., was sent to study in Rome. Disturbed by the profligate life of the city he fled to Subiaco to become a hermit. He was about twenty then, the same age as I,

9

and within a short time the other hermits chose Benedict as their leader. According to legend, some monks became so dissatisfied with his strict standards they tried to poison him. Miraculously, the poisoned cup flew from his hands and smashed onto the floor; hence Benedict's symbol.

But what most interested me was that Benedict never became a priest, nor did most monks in that age. Not until the Middle Ages did literate, wealthy monks becomes priests, bishops and government advisors. Only poor, illiterate monks who did manual labor remained brothers. Adelheim accepted this system of feudal categories. Others, such as Brother Amos, advocated a return to the original ideal.

Amos was a complex and intriguing character. He'd spent his adolescence in Boys' Town after some scrape with the law. I assumed he'd come here, like most monks, to escape the world's corruption. He was brilliant in language and philosophy but his demeanor was hardly pious. Once, asked to translate a certain Greek text overnight, he responded: "That would be about as easy as deballing the abbot."

Presiding over Latin class, Amos made the dead language leap with relevance. He'd tell salacious anecdotes, crack sexual jokes about Cicero and others whose work we studied. More disconcerting was his habit of poking me in the ribs.

Sometimes he'd join me on the portico as I watched younger seminarians frolic on the lawn below. "What I'd give for that one to leap on my back," he'd say, winking, or: "I'd bet getting a kiss from Robbie would be like flying to Heaven in a chariot." When my jaw would tighten he'd nudge me again and say, "*Summum quam bonum.* There's no beauty like a beautiful face in prayer." Then I'd feel an even greater consternation.

What bothered me was that Robbie reminded me of a kid in my grade school catechism class. Jamie was slender like me but full of life and always getting in trouble with Sister Madeline. She'd make him bend over and whip him in front of class. Above them hung the usual swooning Jesus. This combination of images thrilled me and I ached to know what Jamie would look like taking his punishment naked. I even dreamt of it once, of carrying his bruised sweaty body out to the cemetery where my father lay. Under the wisteria I kissed his wounds.

So it wasn't just Robbie's attractiveness which bothered me but the unexpected force of memory, this and hearing Amos speak as if to tie me into some lewd conspiracy of his own. Above everything I valued privacy. The more Amos talked, the more I armored myself against him.

One afternoon, as I was shelving some books of Jung, Amos came upon me. "Jung!" he exclaimed, raising his eyebrows like someone who's just found a lost drachma, "Have you ever read his appendix on the Dance of the Virgin Mary?" When I confessed I hadn't, he proceeded to fill me in. Suddenly he embraced me. The pores and scratchy stubble of his unshaven, oily face pressed against my cheek, his vice-like arms squeezed me. Enveloped in his sweaty robe, I felt I was falling into a grave. Terrified, I pushed him away. What if someone saw us? I ran from the library and avoided Amos as best I could for the next several days, Finally, he cornered me.

"Hey, I wasn't trying to rape you," he said with characteristic directness. "The Kiss of Peace has been part of the Mass since the first century. What's the big fuss?"

"We weren't in Mass," I replied crossly. "We were in the stacks of the library."

"Well, God saw us and we're still alive aren't we?" Amos nailed me with his eyes. "Okay, I'm sorry you misunderstood. If you don't want to be hugged fine, but we don't have to become strangers, do we?"

I agreed I'd maybe overreacted but kept more distance from Amos just the same. And yet, I found myself occasionally nudging other young seminarians in the ribs. If a monk as brilliant as Amos saw no harm in this, why should a newcomer like me feel uptight? I didn't think I could safely discuss this matter with Adelheim but began looking for someone else I could talk to.

About this time I met Mort Halpern who sat in front of me during Compline. This exercise was held in the largest room in our dorm. Folding chairs sat in military rows with an aisle leading down the center to a large wooden podium emblazoned with a painted Christos, a capital **P** over an **X**. Waiting for one of our prefects to arrive, Father Theodosius or Ezekiel, I meditated on this symbol. Was the **P** arising, phoenix-like, from the **X**, or was the **X** trying to bind the **P** in a prison of physical suffering?

One night I noticed that Mort's adam's apple looked not unlike the **P** of the Christos. He was tall and skinny with piercing dark eyes and an unkempt thatch of brown hair. Good and evil were absolutely clear to him yet ninety percent of the pranks in St. Christopher's Hall were of his doing. His fanaticism stirred my interest.

On July 25th, our dorm's feast day, a party was scheduled in the canteen after Compline. Although not in a mood for socializing, I followed the crowd of seminarians downstairs and found myself sitting with Halpern, Paganini and a couple others from Amos's Latin class.

Paganini, an enormously fat and foul-mouthed kid from the Bronx, was obsessed with collecting gold and silver rosaries. The year before he'd instigated a "Miss Conception" contest for which he'd decked himself out in a bridal gown made from an Irish linen tablecloth his mother had sent him. He was also prone to writing limericks such as

There once was a quaint old monk
Whose cum smelled not unlike skunk.
He prayed to the Lord
for a better reward
and awakened to find his tool shrunk.

To say the least, Paganini's incessant jabbering irritated me. Tonight he was arguing that it was okay for him to eat four dishes of ice cream since he'd lost ten pounds on his diet.

"Marxists have a saying for that," I mused. "It's called uneven and combined development."

Halpern exploded in laughter. "You're an odd one, Armand," he exclaimed. "You shouldn't hide your light under a bushel basket."

"It's also written: 'Don't throw your pearls before swine,'" I replied, pleased that he'd noticed me. After a bit more such banter I went upstairs to our attic bunkroom but was surprised to find Halpern following me. He drew me aside into an empty study hall.

"You seem an okay guy so I should warn you," he confided. "Something's not right about this place."

"You mean how Paganini acts?"

Halpern laughed.

"That, too, but I'm talking about something else." His eyes narrowed. "There's evil brewing here, a feud between God and Satan." I thought of the contradictory spiritual advice our prefects gave but "evil" and "Satan" seemed pretty strong words.

On Monday, Wednesday and Friday evenings, Father Theodosius would address us. He was about fifty, walked with a cane, and looked like a pelican only 200 pounds heavier. Born of British aristocracy, he'd just returned form five years at the Gregorian Institute in Rome. Rome! The very way he rolled the word over his tongue as he peered at us through his spectacles evoked learning, tradition, discipline. Abbot Placid has assigned him to our dorm to put him back in touch with American reality.

"Gentleman," he'd begin, rapping the side of the podium with his cane. "It is my mind and the mind of Holy Mother Church . . ." and off he'd go on some tangent such as "Cleanliness is next to Godliness." If we were to be shining examples of Faith, we must fastidiously imitate Christ in all respects, particularly in regard to such often neglected details as manicuring our finger-nails.

On alternate nights, Father Ezekiel would come before us. Equal in size to Theodosius, Zeke was his opposite in every other respect. A high school dropout from Denver, Zeke was Inviolate's resident beatnik. His art room was filled with junk he'd stolen from nearby abandoned farmhouses: odd bits of furniture, boxes of old magazines and clothes, pipes and machine parts — all this he'd arranged into a giant still life which grew more convoluted with every passing year. I'd heard he'd once startled a freshman English class by pulling down the shades and singing "Frankie and Johnnie Were Lovers . . . ."

"Be yourselves," Father Zeke would say. "Hang loose. How can we dig this 'Freedom in Christ' bit till we've learned to be like those lilies of the field? Why should God want a bunch of neurotics running around in his name?"

The next night Theodosius would return. "You must *work* for salvation," he'd scream. "Nothing good comes easy." The light from the etched glass light fixture dangling from the ceiling bounced off his glasses like fire. So it would go, back and forth, but this different spiritual emphasis between two dorm prefects seemed hardly the stuff of a monastic feud.

"I'm serious," Halpern insisted. "I've heard some of the younger monks in Zeke and Amos's faction hold . . ." — and here his voice became deathly earnest — "homosexual *orgies!*"

"And where do they do this," I laughed nervously. "In the crypt?"

While Halpern's charge upset me, I couldn't help recalling a funny story Amos had told me about the crypt shortly after I'd met him. This room was situated under the main altar of the basilica. A dozen niches along its damp stone walls were outfitted with small altars. Since every priest had to celebrate Mass once a day, freshman seminarians had to get up early to serve those monks who didn't go into the surrounding parishes to say Mass. One was a gruff ex-Trappist nicknamed Beartracks. He was quite an object of mystery since he spoke but once a year and then, only when required to deliver a sermon before the whole congregation.

One morning, Beartracks noticed a new seminarian trembling as he handed him his alb. Beartracks kept silent till fully vested. Then he turned to the lad, lifted his arms in a horror movie gesture, and growled: "Take me to the crypt." The poor seminarian was so startled he wet his pants.

Halpern snorted.

"Okay, laugh if you want to. You're the one planning to be a monk, not me. I just thought you'd be someone who took the idea of hell seriously, who wouldn't go gaga over that crap about saving your soul by reading psychology. There might be more going on in that crypt than you realize."

"Are you proposing to be my spiritual advisor?" Halpern's intimate, personal concern over my spiritual well-being intrigued me. He bristled for a second, then relaxed.

"I don't know why, Armand, but I like you. You're such an odd duck. Wanna go for a walk tomorrow?"

"Starting off with a heavy dose of penance, I see."

At this I reached over and pinched him. Halpern flinched but I intuited that the gesture secretly pleased him, especially when he began slugging me hard in the arm. Suddenly the study door opened. A shaft of light revealed Father Theodosius standing before us.

"Night silence began fifteen minutes ago, gentlemen. You are expected to observe it." As we sheepishly filed past him I felt oddly uncomfortable. Part of my embarrassment was to have been caught breaking a rule, something I was loath to do, but something more

15

bothered me. Although Theodosius was standing behind us so I couldn't see his face, I felt as if he was lasciviously touching me with his eyes.

As the summer passed, Halpern and I became increasingly close. Some of my studiousness began rubbing off on him. After Latin class each morning, we'd work together on our assignments memorizing a passage of Cicero or Augustine. After lunch, we'd take off on long walks through the fields.

Walking with Halpern and listening to his stories I felt exhilaratingly boyish. Unlike Trollson, my only previous close friend, Halpern loved to tease and roughhouse. His laugh, which convulsed his whole body like hiccups, was contagious. Sometimes we'd roll on the ground laughing our heads off about things I can no longer recall.

Mostly Halpern told me about Beartracks, how in winter he'd scoop snow off the baseball field wearing nothing but summer slacks and a tee shirt, or how in summer he'd don a heavy parka and bicycle twenty miles or more. Beartracks, even more than Theodosius, was his model of saintliness. Halpern was also the first to tell me why Ezekiel was abruptly transferred to an Indian mission that summer.

While Zeke was attending a weekend art conference in Kansas City, Theodosius cleaned out his art room. Zeke's cherished still life was dismantled and burned. When Zeke returned and discovered this, he calmly went up to Theodosius's second floor office and threw everything out the window. Among those objects was a history of Inviolate Theodosius was working on in which Abbot Placid figured prominently.

What Halpern didn't discuss was the orgies he'd first warned me about. One afternoon I reminded him.

"There's two kinds of monks here," he said, reddening. "Lovers and Haters. It's the Lovers you have to watch out for. Since you were new here, I just thought I should warn you."

"Isn't it dangerous to spread gossip without proof? As for 'Lovers,' I thought that's what we were supposed to be as Christians."

Halpern took a cattail out of his mouth and tossed a small stone into the lake. Some forty yards away a young brother monk I didn't know sat in a rowboat tugging at a fishing line. Halpern paid no attention. He looked at me with a dark seriousness.

"Maybe Amos never made a pass at you but he has me. And not just me either. One night I was walking alone through the cemetery when I saw him with that kid Robbie. They were . . . ."

"Well, they were what?"

"They were *kissing!*"

Halpern spat out the word so ferociously I thought he might hit me. Hit me, in fact, he often did. On walks I'd often poke him and he'd get so mad he'd throw me on the ground and either hit or tickle me till I cried "Uncle." This is just what I wanted. The more he wrestled, the pokier I became. I loved the feel of his taut skinny legs pressing my shoulders into the earth, the heat of his Viking breath blasting me in the face. What else I wanted I wasn't sure. A more emotional or intellectual closeness? I tried to talk to him about literature of philosophy, but Halpern spurned all attempts at serious discussion.

"Philosophy's the work of the devil," he'd snort, his Adam's apple bouncing up and down on his throat like a Moveable Feast. "Most fuckups around here don't take the Bible seriously. They think philosophy and psychology have made the concept of hell old-fashioned. Well, they'll get a rude awakening come Judgement Day."

His eyes looked fiercer than ever, just as they looked at me now. What I wanted, I realized, was exactly what he considered the ultimate evil — a fiery kiss from his lips, a kiss to release his pent-up wrath. Let him ravage and burn himself out on me like a volcano so that, together, we might melt into God.

As if he'd read my mind, Halpern bounded up in one

leap. "This conversation's getting too weird. In fact I'm beginning to think *you're* getting too weird." Before I could reply he stomped off.

The more I sought Halpern out the next few days, the more he avoided me. Exasperated, I finally wrote him a note which I slipped into his Latin book where he'd be sure to find it. "Friendship with you is like dancing on a tightrope of razorblades. Why won't you talk to me any more? Surely it's no sin to be friends. Think of Jesus and John." I signed the note with that most fatal of words, "love," and my name.

Henceforth, Halpern refused to have anything to do with me. A terrible emptiness swelled in my belly and all the pleasures I previously felt fell away. Inviolate's fresh baked bread had no more taste, its fields and lake no more allure, theological magazines no more interest. No images of hell Halpern brandished were as horrid as his simple absence.

But greater still was the pain of seeing him deteriorate. Although never a good student, he started skipping classes and hanging out with his former archenemy, Paganini. His language coarsened. I heard via the dorm grapevine that they were sneaking out at night to see girls in nearby Thomasville. One night they returned drunk, Halpern singing off key at the top of his lungs. I knew he'd be kicked out if this kept up but what could I do? At my last attempt to talk to him his eyes glazed over like a frightened baby rabbit's. Never had I seen anyone so miserable. Rejecting me, he felt it necessary to reject everything I stood for. Finally I went to Amos, the only monk I thought I could trust with this problem.

"You would have to have chosen Halpern," Amos sighed. "Well, I'll see what I can do. Maybe I can get Beartracks to talk to him — if Beartracks will talk to anyone that is."

But it was too late. That night Theodosius waddled into Compline with an unusually self-satisfied smile.

"I have a most unpleasant announcement," he

began, pausing to bask in our undivided attention. When he was sure he had it he continued. "One of our number, Morton S. Halpern, has just been expelled."

My heart sank. Disjointed phrases wafted over the empty chair in front of me: "Grievous errors . . . departed form the priestly path . . . the devil creeps about like a wily lion seeking whom to devour . . . a lesson to us all."

Halpern had refused to identify his "cohorts in sin," as Theodosius put it. The phrase stuck in my throat. More than ever I blamed myself for Mort's downfall which, though I'd tried mightily, I'd been helpless to stop. But why had no one seen him leave?

"Maybe he was too ashamed to say goodbye," Amos mused later. That made sense. Getting kicked out must have been the most devastating humiliation of his life. More than anything Mort had wanted to be a priest. I couldn't imagine him fitting into society in any other way.

I felt dizzy, numb. The final words of Theodosius's announcement rang in my ears with an ironic mockery: "The sacred writers related the vicious as well as virtuous actions of men which have this moral effect, that it keeps mankind from despair."

# Two

Fall passed into Winter, then Spring. It could have been epochs as far as I was concerned for thoughts of Halpern haunted me like a severed limb. I redoubled my studies, reading all of Kafka during this time, but my stay at Inviolate was making me jaded. Father Raymond's basilica no longer seemed so innocent and delightful. At least one fourth of the monks suffered ulcers

Surely my feeling, my desire for friendship was evil or it wouldn't have caused so much harm, not only to myself but to others. Was this the result of an arrested emotional development or something worse? About this time I met Father Bonaventure. He was tall, brilliant and regal in every movement. He was also Black and one of the handsomest men I'd ever seen. He'd come from the Bahamas for Inviolate's Pastoral Institute.

The Institute was organized to teach priests and monks about the Second Vatican Council which was still in progress. Pope John's spiritual advisor, Bernard Häring, was teaching a course on Moral Theology, and Abbot Lawrencius Klein from Germany a course on Ecumenism. Everyone but me was excited to be meeting these historic Church leaders.

I'd already talked to Bonaventure several times in the library so it wasn't hard for me to arrange to meet him alone for an evening walk. He was one of the few monks I'd met who was as well-versed in Existentialism and modern literature as in Patristics and Medieval Theology. If anyone could help me resolve my sexual dilemma, surely it was he. For days I pondered how to raise the question, finally deciding to present it in the form of an allegory which had been turning in my mind for some time. We left the refectory, passed the statue of St. Joseph in front of the print shop, and headed toward the cemetery and the road to Thomasville. I began:

### The Allegory

*Hidden in a deep forest lay a town without music. No radios. No record players. No musical instruments of any kind. One day a stranger arrived wearing black gloves and carrying a violin. How sad everyone looks, he thought. No one knows how to whistle. Not even birds sing. But the townspeople were kind enough to give him food and shelter so he wanted to give something in return. He announced he had a special gift for everyone, something wonderful, so the townspeople assembled to see what it was.*

*Imagine how surprised they were. How delighted, at the sound of the stranger's violin. "Tap, tap," went their feet and smiles broke forth on their faces. As if by magic the town was transformed. Soon the stranger became the town's most popular person and the mayor's daughter fell in love with him. They agreed to marry. Despite the girl's love, however, one quirk of the stranger bothered her. "Why don't you ever remove your gloves?"*

*The stranger paled. "How I'd love to touch you, to caress your lovely face," he said mournfully. "But I cannot nor can I explain why. If I removed my gloves you'd love me no more. So I beg you, never discuss this again." Perplexed, the stubborn girl decided if he wouldn't take off his gloves, she would after their wedding.*

21

*The wedding day arrived and the stranger
played his violin with more feeling and beauty
than ever before. Then his bride said cheerfully,
"Put down your violin a moment, my husband.
Let's dance." As he did so, she quickly pulled
off his right glove.*

*Instead of a hand, even a misshapen hand,
a writhing, leafy vegetable spilled from his
sleeve. Revolted, the girl screamed. Looking to
see what was wrong, the townspeople took up
her cry. The stranger was driven away amid
many blows and curses and music was heard
no more in that land.*

Bonaventure looked at me quizzically. It was almost
dark now, that moment of twilight when edges are
blurred as by a brushtroke. We stood alone in the
cemetery. Cicadas droned. Here and there, fireflies blinked
like stars.

"So what are you trying to say?" Bonaventure asked.
I poured out my confusion at Amos's advances, my pain
at Halpern's rejection.

"What should I do, Father? Everything I read about
homosexuality's so vague and clinical that it doesn't
seem to fit my experience at all." *Homosexual!* The word
spilled out like the monstrous leaf from the stranger's
sleeve. Bonaventure laughed. His voice was deep, com-
forting, but I was afraid to look into his eyes.

"You're not so unique. Don't you know almost
everyone has these feelings sometimes?" As if to prove
his point, he slipped his hands under my tee shirt and
around my waist. "Your waist is like a woman's," he
whispered, pulling me toward him.

I froze. What I'd wanted was advice, not a seduc-
tion. I was fond of Bonaventure but the unexpected
feeling of his hands inside my clothes was a shock.
Thinking quickly of an excuse, I bolted from him, my

inner turmoil greater than ever.

Now, a week later, I sat on a hard wooden bench between the long row of blue spruces west of St. Christopher's, my sleepy mind trying to make sense of my problems. What was I doing at a monastery anyway? Could I remain here as confused as I was?

Not only was the bench shaded, it was perched on the bluff above the handball courts where it enjoyed a slight breeze. Elsewhere, heat not only beat down from the sun but rose from the ground like the spirts of vengeful Sioux warriors massacred here long ago. Halpern had told me that an arrowhead once punctured the front tire of Beartracks' bike. Falling forward over the vehicle, he'd seen a vision of the Ghost Dancers. Had this really happened?

I shut my eyes and tried to imagine Ghost Dancers rising before me. Instead Paganini floated up, his buck teeth parted in a Bronx guffaw. He was fiddling with what seemed to be the controls of a spacecraft but which looked more like stereo equipment. When not eating, Paganini's head was wrapped in earphones.

"Twenty minutes to take-off," he intoned, cocking his head sideways as if listening to his master's voice. Then I saw others stringing onto the craft: Tom Sutton who'd sold insurance to Bob Hope and other celebrities before entering the seminary, B.J. Bird whose adages Paganini was collecting into a notebook. Most were about monastery food, sayings such as, "If you can't name it, don't eat it."

Adelheim, Theodosius and Beartracks trooped on board, their hooded heads bowed. Then came Amos and Bonaventure arm in arm. Finally those I'd known at Milo such as Trollson climbed onto the bright metallic stairway. Although far away I could hear plainly what everyone said.

"All aboard?" Theodosius scurried about like a worried hen. "Let's take off before the deluge."

"Come on," Amos cried, waving his arm. "What are

23

you waiting for?"

I try to move but can't — no, I *am* moving. I'm running as fast as I can but getting nowhere. I'm breathless, my mouth is dry. Pain stabs my side from running so hard but I'm not moving. "Armand!" everyone cries as the stairway starts to rise. Behind me I hear Halpern laughing fiendishly, then another voice, one I'd never head before.

"Armand, can I talk to you?"

Opening my eyes, I saw a figure silhouetted against the sun. Wispy ends of blond hair shimmered blindingly. Such perfect eyebrows, such delicate features, such deep set, sparkling eyes. Jacob confronting his angel couldn't have been more stunned. I felt nonplussed, afraid to speak. Up close, Robbie Warfield's beauty scared me. It was too perfect. I squinted, turned to look down at toy-sized figures on the ballfield. My sweaty tee shirt stuck uncomfortably to my back.

"Whadaya wanna talk about?"

"I think I know how you've been feeling. I had a friend in Chicago once who did a lot of neat stuff, helped homeless kids get on their feet. One day a kid turned him in for supposedly making a pass at him."

"What's that got to do with me?"

The drift of Robbie's conversation was making me nervous and I avoided looking at him. I wound a cattail tightly around my finger to anchor myself.

"I wasn't just talking about you," Robbie laughed. "We're connected. We both want to become monks right?" He didn't mean to be forward, Robbie said, but he knew Halpern and I had been close. He thought I'd been good for Mort and shouldn't blame myself that he'd been kicked out. It hurt him to see me withdraw because a lot of people needed me.

"*Need* me?" My cynicism convinced me I wasn't dreaming.

"You brighten people up in ways I could never do. You touch their minds." Robbie took my hand. Over

24

mine, his felt soft as velvet. A small scar on his thumb showed white against his tan. I felt angry to have been caught off guard but Robbie didn't seem to notice.

"I've wanted to meet you for a long time but didn't know what to say. I thought you'd think I was hopelessly dumb or something."

For awhile we sat silently. Now I knew why Robbie was so well-liked by some, yet hated by others. His naivete. Everything Halpern had cursed me for, he was praising me for. I slapped at a mosquito which had landed on my neck.

"It's okay if you touch me," Robbie said, stroking my bare arm. "I need love too. We all do. It's stupid to pretend we don't." Robbie was so close I could feel his breath. The smell of his sweat sharpened the pollen-laden air. I looked at him now and saw his eyes were sad too, blue, and deep with a loneliness; he had a vulnerable openness I'd never seen before.

I won't relate the rest of what we did that evening except to say I awakened from a very long sleep. Morning was bright again and robins sang with a clarity I'd forgotten. All my senses felt cleansed. The smell of scrambled eggs and toast hit my nostrils as I walked downstairs from the basilica after Mass. Robbie was setting metal pitchers of milk on the tables. His smile was as bright as the white apron he wore.

When Father Theodosius came in and rang the bell, everyone sat down. All was silent except for a subdued clinking of silverware and a seminarian reading to us about the life of some long dead saint. But it was living saints I was concerned with. I glanced back to where Robbie sat. He winked.

Classes that day seemed longer than usual. Latin droned endlessly. In philosophy, Father Adelheim lectured on John Scotus Eriugena and the Emanating One but creatures as participations and theophanies didn't interest him. He was impatient to move into the more logical world of Thomas Aquinas. In Gregorian chant,

25

poor Father Raymond couldn't remember what questions he'd been asked by the time he turned around to write them on the blackboard. Finally lunchtime came and the afternoon was ours.

We headed up the dirt road to Thomasville, a road bounded on one side by a rustic, weathered fence and the monastery cattle pasture, and on the other, by a narrow strip of trees and still more farms. Often I'd walked here with Halpern, Bonaventure, or even alone. It was here, in fact, that I'd first seen Robbie. He'd been sitting on the fence wearing a tee shirt and black slacks, cassocks being reserved only for Mass and classes. He'd smiled, then for no apparent reason, bounded off over the fields. In the distance he looked like a romping faun but his face had burned itself into my mind like stigmata. Even then I knew he was unusual. His ankles blazed in bright red socks instead of fading in traditional monastic black.

"Why'd you run off the first time I saw you?"

"Maybe I was scared of your beauty." Robbie grinned mischievously. I knew he was joking but in what sense? Did he mean I was foolish to be so impressed by his looks or that I was foolish to think he was any more beautiful in my eyes than I was in his?

"Armi," Robbie said, seeing my furrowed brow. "You think too much. Tell me something interesting. What kind of childhood did you have?"

As we climbed the fence and headed over a hill of pasture, I told him briefly about New Orleans. When I shut my eyes and look back as far as I can see in all that blackness, I see only lots of greys, reds, green-bluish, a large white house, a cemetery. The house may not have been large. I was only four when Father died and I was left all alone with Mother, a beautiful, cruel and confused woman.

The cemetery wasn't far from our house. Often I crawled through a secret opening in some lilacs where one of the wrought-iron bars was missing. How Spanish the Spanish moss looked, soft and grey as the weeping willows which wept langorously over a small lake. Here I played amongst clumps of pampas grass and kudzu-covered trees. Here I was left alone with no one to scold or torment me. Here, in my favorite spot by the lake where the sun shone down through the willows, they buried him.

All I recall about Dad is that he read me the Bible. Then he was so alive. His eyes would blaze, his mouth quiver, and when he got to the part where God smote down his enemies, he would sweep his arm through the air like a scythe. I loved my father desperately but feared him at the same time. He was like God: distant, imperious, deep. Then, like God, he was gone.

I loved my mother too but she did not love me. "That child is a curse," she'd scream. "He's just like his father. He haunts me." Over and over I was told this: haunt haunt haunt hurt haunt. Mother was tall too with mint julep eyes and hair like Spanish moss only thick and dark like mine. Grandmother said she was part Cherokee. She smelled of roses and tobacco, Southern Comfort and the pills she took. When father died she took to bed. I tried every way possible to serve her, to inspire in her breast a maternal affection but to no avail.

When I was ten, mother sent me to live with father's parents in Iowa. At first I felt homesick but gradually, by all outward appearances, I became a normal boy, as normal as the elm trees which hung listlessly over pot-holed streets like cornsilk over ears of corn. Grandpa fussed and fumed a lot while Grandma just laughed, her skinny arms shaking in a brown plaid housedress. "Everybody's tetched but me and thee and sometimes I even wonder about thee." Robbie laughed at how I mimicked Grandma's voice. High above me she stood. What a clean smell! A whiff of perfume on Ivory soap. If cleanliness was next to godliness, the three of us lived in heaven.

Robbie's childhood in Chicago was much grimmer: tenements, filth, winos and junkies passed out under the roar of the El. His mother's boyfriends beat him up, sometimes so badly the neighbors called the police and he was taken to a hospital. When he was eight, his mother abandoned him. He came home from school to find everything gone — the furniture, everything. "She didn't even leave a note saying goodbye," Robbie said. "There was just a pile of my clothes on the floor."

For a while he lived on the streets and ate out of garbage cans. He was too hurt to tell anyone what had happened. Then he was picked up and put out for adoption, but his adopted parents died in a car accident when he was twelve. Out on the streets again he was picked up by a pimp and locked in a closet till he was so hungry he was willing to do anything. To keep him pliable the pimp hooked him on heroin. At fourteen Robbie was arrested and sent to reform school. How had these cruel experiences not crushed or embittered him?

"Only we who've suffered most for love can understand how important it is to give love back to the world."

I wanted to scoff. Robbie's comment sounded too much like the moral tacked onto saints' lives: Agatha, for instance, whose breasts were plucked off and who was subsequently pictured in Church art carrying them in a dish. Their resemblance to bells led to her adoption as patron saint of bell-founders; their resemblance to round loaves to a custom of blessing bread in church on her feast day. Yes, about as uplifting as TV dramas on concentration camps punctuated by soap commercials. I'd had enough of "naive" goodness.

"Weren't you angry?"

"God didn't create us to be miserable and angry," Robbie continued. He insisted that any experience, no matter how terrible, could be somehow redeemed by surrounding it with God's love. And then — but why not tell you. Robbie would have wanted you to know.

When you're in love with someone who's equally in love with you, sometimes just a glance is fulfilling. When, added to this, you and your beloved are dedicated to the same goal — to increase love in the world — then the thrill of mutual devotion may be greater than any sexual touch. But often, too, because of past physical or emotional deprivation, a sexual sharing is needed or desired. When this happens, and when you and your lover are so close that a need felt by one is immediately felt as a need of both, then truly you've tasted heaven.

It's funny, even as I write this, I don't know if Robbie was homosexual or not. I asked him once and he said, "Why are you so concerned with labels? Love can't be labeled. It just is."

So why do I ponder this now? What I can say with certainty is this.

Robbie's lips were neither irritatingly aggressive or guiltily shy. When we kissed we felt we were flying, our arms and legs like wings as we covered each other with kisses. Robbie felt my hungers as if they were his and in the same way I felt his. We began to live not so much *for* each other as *through* each other, as if each of us were a mirror in which we could see each other more deeply.

Sometimes Robbie'd moan, "O come inside me Armand. I want us to be totally inside each other like the angels are," or "Drink me. I want to give you all of myself." And next to his lithe body stretched out in the sun, or luminous in the damp grass when we met at night, I knew what Moses must have felt after his long trek through Egypt.

"Bite my nipples," Robbie'd say, or "No, let me do you this time." And he'd spring up on his knees and swoop down on my cock like a kid on his first ice cream cone. Everything possible to do with each other sexually we did and sometimes we'd make love again and again until we were both utterly exhausted. Other times we'd simply hold each other and look at the sky.

Of course no love is perfect. Often I wished Robbie were more intellectual, that he could enjoy books as well as people. For instance, Mrs. Zurfis, a widow with arthritis who lived in a farmhouse between Inviolate and

Thomasville, did laundry for the monastery. Instead of studying, Robbie would help her. Listening to her gossip wasn't so bad but her litany of health complaints bored me silly.

"She's just lonely," Robbie'd say. "Cheering her up is more important than reading any book."

"You're just encouraging her hypochondria," I'd reply. "She'll snap one of these days and drown herself in all that holy water you bring her."

Other friends of Robbie's, such as Amos, made me jealous. Robbie swore their friendship wasn't sexual but what Halpern said about them stuck in my mind. I knew how aggressive Amos could be and the thought of anyone's tongue but mine in Robbie's mouth drove me mad.

"Jealousy's stupid," Robbie'd say peevishly. "If you can't believe I'm giving myself to you as much as humanly possible . . ." and he looked so forlorn I hated myself for ever doubting him. But worst of all was Robbie's stubborn lack of discretion.

If he felt like holding a friend's hand during Mass, he would. If he felt like kissing a nun friend on the lips in front of the basilica, he would. I knew Adelheim and Theodosius were increasingly upset at such behavior since they lectured him about it constantly but when Amos told me the matter had come up at Chapter meeting I knew I'd have to talk to Robbie myself. We met in the record room, a seldom-used lounge downhall from the library.

"I know there's nothing *wrong* with what you're doing but is it worth getting kicked out for? Do you have to flaunt spontaneity in front of these guys who've spent fifty years thinking morality's what looks right?"

"How did Christ act? He confronted the Pharisees head on. He said, 'The letter kills but the spirit gives Life.'"

"Nobody's asking you to kill anybody's spirit. I'm just saying let's use a little common sense in how we channel it for a while."

Despite warm, desert brown walls and orange, facing corduroy couches, the record room never felt colder. Drawn out strains of Hohvanhess' *Magic Mountain* did little to abate our gloom. I told Robbie I loved him *because* he was as he was. I said he was right and the others wrong. But what were our long-range goals? Those guys had the power now. Look what they'd done to Ezekiel, to Halpern.

"This place needs us. It needs *you*. Eventually we can change things but not now. Why can't you just cool it awhile? Just for a while that's all I ask."

Robbie looked as if I'd slapped him. I thought at first it was because I'd gotten angry and raised my voice. We'd never really argued before. But that wasn't it, at least not entirely.

"Does that mean . . . Are you saying you don't want to meet me at night any more? Because if you are . . . ." Robbie's voice trembled as he turned to the wall.

"Oh Christ," I cried. "You *know* . . . ." But what did we know? All this time I'd marveled at how mutual our love was, had not a tiny part of me kept fearing he was only my lover because *I* wanted it? And what of his fears? How close people can be and still not know each other. "*Noverim te, noverim me.*" If I could but know you, if I could but know myself.

In the shadows Robbie looked incorporeal. Only the left side of his nose and cheek could be seen clearly, illumined by the glow of a small goosenecked lamp between us. He sat cross-legged pulling at the rust colored shag rug.

"I never had a Dad or older Brother, Armi. You're the first guy I've ever met who's been seriously interested in the real me, the scared, lost little shit nobody else knows. You think it doesn't hurt, what guys like Paganini say behind my back? You think I enjoy upsetting Adelheim and Theodosius?"

Seeing Robbie on the verge of tears upset and angered me. I was tired of problems, tired of this argument we were having now. Everyone suffered, so what? Then a new dilemma dawned on me. What would *I* do if they kicked Robbie out?

"Theodosius is a tortured man," Robbie continued. "He's got the worst case of ulcers around. But when's it going to stop if not now? Who's going to change things if not us? What's Amos or anyone accomplished around here with their so-called common sense?"

"Shit," I said, lighting a cigarette. "Guess if you get kicked out we can join Zeke on that reservation." Robbie looked up at me, his eyes wide. "Well wake up. Amos says they're about to do just that. It's already come up at Chapter."

"The Lovers versus the Haters," Robbie murmured softly. I don't think I'd ever seen him quite so solemn. For a long time neither of us spoke. It was as if the "real world" had struck a giant mailed fist through the window and knocked us on our asses. We were shaken to the core. Had it changed our love too? Finally Robbie began talking, slowly, deliberately, so as to avoid tears.

"At first I thought you were angry with me Armand and it felt . . . it felt like the whole universe was angry. I don't know what I'd do if you rejected me. And I don't know what I'd do if I couldn't become a monk." He looked so fragile, so helpless. Then he began a story that was so amazing I didn't know how to react.

When Robbie was very young, after he was beat up once, he was taken to a Benedictine hospital. His mother visited him, not because she loved him, but because she was afraid the court might take him away and she'd lose her welfare. Then her boyfriend would beat her up too. Robbie knew this but wanted to tell his mother he loved her anyway only he couldn't. His jaw was wired shut. So his mother left. At this Robbie stopped and looked at me strangely.

"Armand, I had a vision of Jesus. I thought maybe I'd died and gone to heaven but He said no, I hadn't, because He had a job for me to do. He wanted me to be a monk someday like the ones who were taking care of me. He wanted me to spread love in the world like He'd done and He said He wouldn't come for me again till I'd done my job."

Robbie curled his legs up under his chin and looked as if he was five years old again. I wasn't sure if I should let him go on. For some reason I was becoming anxious.

"I know what you're thinking but I have to tell someone. Who would that be if not you?"

"You mean you haven't even told Father Adelheim? Maybe if you explained this to him, or to Abbot Placid . . . ."

"But they're not believers in this stuff. Not really. They'd want a sign and that's not what I'm supposed to do." Robbie sighed. "I'm scared, Armand. I need to be with you tonight. I need you now more than I ever needed anyone. I never knew our friendship would get so heavy."

"Me neither," I replied honestly. Either Robbie was absolutely crazy, or . . .

"And it's the 'or' that's the heaviest, isn't it?"

Robbie smiled, amused at my reaction to his reading my mind. He took my hand and put it over his heart. I could feel it beating fast as his blue eyes sucked me up into their infinity.

"I want you to promise one thing. Swear you'll never repeat what I've just said."

"Never?"

"Not for at least fifteen years," Robbie laughed. To humor him I swore. I also agreed to meet him later that night.

# Three

Snow is never white. It mixes with dust and pollution from the very moment of its inception until when it hits ground, even in the most remote countryside, its whiteness is as inevitably mottled as those third grade diagrams of the soul perforated by tiny pinpricks of venial sin. In industrial areas, snow is black yet we persist in imagining it according to its supposedly original state. So it is with everything we see. We become like the vain water nymph at Salmacia who, spying the hapless Hermaphroditus and having nothing better to do, threw all manner of metaphor over the boy. "She was ready to throw her arms around his *snowy* neck," Ovid tell us, and the result was a fusion that enervated both forever. Had I done this with Robbie or he with me?

Waiting in the snow for him, I considered all the ways I'd known Robbie till now. From the pinnacles of Romance he fell to earth. I'd tasted and squeezed his salty skin. It was not ivory. I'd smelled his armpits, his breath, his farts. They were not ambrosia. I'd memorized every downy hair, every vein and freckle on his body. It was not a map of heaven. In time, I'd come to love Robbie's imperfections even more than his perfections because "perfect" means nothing unless there's some goal to be aspired to, some irregularity to give order its shape and definition.

Robbie's teeth, for instance, weren't quite straight and his lips couldn't pout so charmingly had it not been for his slight overbite. Nor would his arms, which perpetually moved in a sibilant of curves, have so moved me had it not been for the random dispersal of freckles spread over them. I pictured him lying in the grass looking up at me, the stem of a cattail in his mouth. Friend, lover, brother — how quickly the terms we used for each other changed. How quickly Robbie himself changed. Even now, after knowing him for almost a year, did I really see him for who he was?

Although Easter was only two weeks away, a light snow had been falling all afternoon. "A deeper peace than sorrow can ever know," Gabriel Marcel had called Faith in his lecture two weeks earlier. Easy for him to say. He was old and preparing to die. Robbie'd squirmed uncomfortably as the famous Existentialist spoke. Lectures bored him. Classes bored him. Only when we talked did ideas come alive for him.

During Summer and Fall it had been easy for us to slip away into some field after night silence. Who could ever find us in all that darkness. But with the advent of snow our silhouettes stood out and our footprints betrayed us so we began meeting inside. In the attic storeroom of the Theology building we moved some boxes to make a little room in the corner. Inside we spread a grey woollen blanket. Although the dust made us sneeze, we loved this secret cubbyhole with the passion of kids. For awhile we'd discuss the day's events, then we'd give in to the conversation of our bodies.

What is more eloquent than the first speech of fingers, the gentle coming together of hands as if the hand represented the whole human spirit? Or what more instructive than to savor the minute yet vast differences between a fingernail drawn delicately down one's side or a fluttering swim of fingertips down one's back? Different pressures of touch told us who we were too and how our bodies lived in the world. It thrilled me to feel Robbie shudder, to know the ecstasy I was giving him as I moved my tongue lightly around the head of his cock.

Sometimes we also met in the rare book room to which I still had a key. But making love in a rare book room is not without its perils. Any sound over a whisper might be heard in the hall or in the library reading room. One careless kick and a Gutenberg Bible might come crashing down breaking not only its, but *our* precious spines. Still the very danger of our meetings heightened our senses. To go down on each other amidst so many sacred books added a peculiarly religious, even ritualistic dimension to our pleasure. All the prophets, saints and early Church Fathers witnessed our union. How fresh, sweet and alive, too, Robbie's cum tasted amid the musty odor of these old tomes.

At first it bothered me to break night silence. Silence allowed one's spirit to breathe free. It allowed one to listen to nature, to one's deeper self, to God. One of my happiest times at Inviolate had been a two-week Silent Retreat that fall. The simplest acts, going on walks or eating a meal, assumed whole new proportions. I'd gaze into each spoonful before eating, realizing in full my dependence on this slice of peach, this morsel of bread.

Have you ever looked carefully at a piece of bread? Countless fibers thin as spiderwebs span each other interlacing into a veritable beehive of nourishment. The simplest bread crust has the unique, dazzling complexity of a snowflake or the Milky Way. That's the real miracle of life. Gratitude flooded through me to rediscover it.

I discovered other miracles too — the sound of fresh milk pouring into my glass, the sound of leaves crackling underfoot or of sparrows chirping as they hopped over dry twigs, the music of a friend's smile. Ah, this *was* something! To learn smiles really can make sounds, sounds as euphonious as a symphony. Filled with the babble of our own voices we're deaf to so much, but in silence, a silence freely chosen and extended, the orchestra of nature makes itself heard. What had I come to a monastery for if not silence?

"Love," Robbie replied. I leaned over and kissed Robbie's shoulder. He was staring up at the ceiling. It was the first time we'd made love inside. "What if a depressed person needs a kind word? Do you think our first talk could have been postponed till the next morning?" The answer, of course, was no. Certain talks can only occur at night because at night one feels more intimate and protected. So silence wasn't for itself but to help us advance in the path of love. Only weren't we often stretching rules more for our own gratification than for any long-range spiritual good?

"There's your Presbyterian grandmother again," Robbie giggled. I had to laugh and admit I felt far more fulfilled under his tutelage than I'd felt the year before under Adelheim's rules. But what would happen to us? I couldn't expect Robbie to hold in his irrepressible nature for long.

Thinking this I heard Robbie's footsteps crunching in the snow. He'd gotten permission to care for Mrs. Zurfis who was ill and I feigned sickness myself. Going to the bunkroom I'd taken Robbie's and my pillows and beat them into a shape that looked vaguely human under an army blanket. We left at separate times and walked the long way round to the bluff so our footprints couldn't be seen. Next to the clump of pines our black parkas wouldn't stand out so much either and anyone aproaching from the monastery would be visible for at least three hundred yards.

Without a word we fell into each others' arms. Our kiss was long. Then we gazed into each others' eyes as if by so doing we could melt the chill of the outside world. Robbie was just 18, five years younger than I, but looking into his eyes I felt he was older, thousands of years older, it seemed, when he was serious like this — or was it just that I felt so much younger in his presence? Even when Robbie was sad, his eyes smiled.

"Robbie," I said finally. "I've decided my vocation to you is deeper even than my vocation to be a monk, but I want you to know if you ever want to separate, I'll love you enough to let you go."

37

"Love doesn't need promises, but if you're worried I can say I'm yours for as long as I live."

From our perch high on the bluff we could see over the football field to the small lake and even the trees and a few farmhouses beyond. In the shadows the snow looked blue, almost purple in places, but where the moon shone down it glistened. It could have been an ocean and the monastery, rising up out of it, a Leviathan. Lights in the distant farmhouses glimmered like drops of water on a sea creature's back.

"I prayed before coming here," Robbie continued. "I asked blessings for us, and for Adelheim and Theodosius too. Our being together is God's will. I know it is because," and he touched my face as he said this, "because I've prayed for someone like you all my life."

How had I doubted him, even for an instant? So guileless, so innocent. One didn't have to sleep on nails, live in a cave, or shovel snow off baseball fields to be a saint. One had only to risk all for love and trust God for the rest. It was so simple. I took off a glove and wiped my nose which was starting to run.

"Let's get naked and make angel wings in the snow," Robbie said suddenly. In a flash he was out of his pants and parka, giggling and tossing snow at me. How quickly his somberness had passed. "Betcha can't catch me," Robbie teased, but I did and enfolded his skinny, naked body within my warm coat. Being less impetuous than he, I'd been reluctant to throw off my own clothes. He wrapped his legs around my waist. Then, from behind us, I heard a shriek.

"SODOMITES! BLASPHEMERS! DEFILERS OF HOLY GROUND!"

Theodosius charged at us like a raging demon. He must have followed Robbie and been hiding behind a tree.

"MAKE A MOCKERY OF HOLY VOWS, WILL YOU? I KNEW I'D CATCH YOU DEVILS IN SIN! TAKE THIS, YOU EVIL SODOMITES!"

The force of his cane on my back knocked us down. He was insane with rage and looked like a golem thrashing at us in his black parka and hooded habit.

"STOP," I yelled, rolling over to escape his blows. "HAVE YOU GONE CRAZY?" Then I realized it was Robbie he was after.

"EVIL, EVIL, EVIL ONE," Theodosius was screaming. Robbie raised his arms, whether in prayer or for protection I couldn't tell, but a sickening crack told me one of his bones had broken under the blows raining down on him. I lunged for the old monk's legs, latched onto one and started to bite, my sole concern to get him off Robbie. But he shook me off. What strength possessed him?

"WICKED, WICKED BOY," Theodosius screeched as he advance don Robbie again. Robbie was scrambling backwards. He tripped. For an instant he was poised in the air as if flying. Then he was over the bluff's edge.

# Four

I became a mad woman. My cries ripped the air like arrows tipped in fire. For two days I could neither eat nor sleep and when tears would no longer flow, I cried out with Dante: "O Death, don't leave me. Look, even alive I look like you."

During moments of lucidity I was questioned by Abbot Placid and the local authorities. Down a long corridor I was taken, down the dark hallway of polished oak floors and spectral white walls. Over a drinking fountain, in an arched niche, hung a picture of Mary. She didn't glow. My legs felt rubbery and I didn't know whose footsteps these were which echoed, echoed in the quiet hall like bowling balls.

Led into Placid's study, I saw his usually ruddy face was also pale. Previously I'd seen him only from a distance. A large majestic figure, he alone seemed to rise above Inviolate's turmoil. Now he looked like a tired banker, weary eyes sunken in a pallid, puffed face. Facing two clumsy leather chairs stood a superbly finished desk, a delicately carved bookcase, and a hawk-footed bookstand on which an ancient Bible stood half open. Black framed photos of monks, both singly and in groups, hung on one wall like class photos. Behind the costly desk hung a large oil painting depicting St. Benedict holding his cracked cup. A thick Persian carpet covered the floor. The room was so dark and quiet I wondered if maybe we were dead instead of Robbie.

A heavy brass floor lamp, the braided stem of which culminated in an inverted bowl-shaped shade of stained glass, cast a greenish tinge on Placid's features, the most prominent of which was a large bottle nose. A thinner man across from him flickered red and yellow as he paced back and forth. Placid coughed and rubbed fat, blond-haired hands together, every so often squeezing them as if trying to crack a walnut.

"Armand," he said finally, with some difficulty. "This is Sheriff Atkins. I want you to tell us in your own words . . . ."

Whose voice answered, echoing a response to their inane questions? Their faces flickered, then the channel changed and I saw Robbie sitting on the rustic fence dangling his legs or Robbie playing leapfrog, tumbling over, his cassock half over his head exposing his pants and strawberry red socks. My mind had no control over where it went. I was returned to my cell.

Amos was appointed to stay with me, no doubt an uneasy duty. Robbie had been taken to the Thomasville mortuary, he said. There something unusual had happened. As old Carl Massie prepared to embalm Robbie, a figure materialized, saying, "Don't touch this boy. I will keep him." Carl was so frightened he refused to do anything but lay Robbie in a coffin. Amos said old Carl was an alcoholic and couldn't be trusted, but the story spread just the same. Monks, seminarians, even townspeople and nearby farmers filled the basilica to overflowing.

Leaning against the narrow window, I gazed through dusty venetian blinds. The sky was grey but looked white against the oak window frame. Below, monks and seminarians gathered in small groups. I imagined their voices, their hushed but excited gossip. Incidents which had attracted little notice before were now re-examined for portentous details.

One story, Amos said, concerned the fact that when Robbie died the basilica bells had started ringing. I was too grief-stricken to notice but they'd clanged away for an hour. No one could explain it. Another story concerned a sermon Beartracks had preached during Holy Week the year before. How well I remembered.

Robbie had dragged me to the front pew where, like everyone, we eagerly awaited what Inviolate's most enigmatic monk would say. Beartracks began a rambling discourse about the most mundane of objects, an empty Coke bottle he'd found in the refectory. Vacantly his wizened eyes wandered the corners of the basilica as if he was seeing it for the first time. Fixing at last on Robbie, they suddenly blazed forth as if to set him on fire.

"What an insignificant thing," Beartracks thundered. "Not even St. Bonaventure would have bothered over such junk. But aren't *we* like this bottle? Haven't *we* been cast aside by a world that considers us useless? But look! Around us, beneath us, above us, yes, even *through* us shines the light of being. BE-ING! What a simple word. But what does it mean? BE-ing, not DO-ing — this is our witness! We are to the Church as the Church is to the world. But what *is* this BE-ing that surrounds us, supports us, inundates and threatens to overwhelm us in our trembling insignificance?"

The old monk stopped, his withered arms helplessly outstretched as he look imploringly around the congregation. He seemed to be pleading for an answer to some overwhelming crisis of his own, a crisis so deep he didn't register where he was. Then the unearthly stillness of the basilica brought him back. Again he looked at Robbie, whose eyes were now lowered, but at that moment Robbie raised his head and looked at Beartracks so firmly and with such an uncanny, ecstatic expression that the monk almost winced as he clutched the sides of the ornate pulpit and appraised the situation quite differently.

"You *know* what this Being is," he stammered in a feverish whisper. Speaking now as if he and Robbie were alone, his voice took on an angelic softness like a fluttering of wings.

"You who so often have been rejected, you *know* the secret of this Being. This Being . . . this BE-ing . . . is

*. . . LOVE!"*

Never had Beartracks delivered such a powerful sermon. Monks and seminarians floated from the basilica as if borne on clouds; yet several later noted how odd it was how the old monk had seemed hypnotized by Robbie. Beartracks had asked to celebrate Robbie's funeral Mass, Amos told me, but Abbot Placid had refused.

I turned from the window. None of my friends was allowed to visit me. I was kept in isolation with Amos my jailer. How ashamed he must have felt. He kept apologizing, chattering constantly to assuage his guilt. I refused to talk and left my food untouched. Pacing from window to door, I gripped my elbows behind my back, wishing I was dead.

Robbie's body was not decomposing, Amos said. It was keeping its color. It was rumored the Apostolic Legate in Washington was coming to investigate. Mrs. Zurfis claimed that Robbie had fixed her breakfast that fatal morning. She swore they joked and gossiped as always. Oh, the stories that circulated.

The monastery's conservative faction pressured to have Robbie buried immediately. Ordinarily a monastery would be greatly honored if one of its novices was sanctified, but in this situation it would obviously create a scandal, not only for the monastery but for the entire Church. What did I care? One moment with my Robbie, living or dead, meant more to me than all the holy cards or miracles in the world. But they wouldn't let me see him. My presence would exacerbate things, they said. I was kept in isolation with Amos my jailer. I was heavily and regularly sedated but the sedatives had no effect.

"Just one glimpse," I begged. "I swear by my eternal soul not to make a scene." Amos nervously rubbed his greasy face.

"Even if I wanted to let you see him, there's no way you could possibly get into the basilica. Placid's posted monks by every door and five around the coffin itself."

"A disguise then," I pleaded. "I could wear a dis-

43

guise."

Amos pondered. I could tell from how he looked at me what price I'd have to pay. Trembling, a cold nausea creeping up my stomach, I slowly approached him. Each step seemed to take an eternity. When I was about a foot away I glanced up at him, then down again. I could feel his hands on my buttocks. I could feel his hands tighten as he pulled me closer. I shut my eyes as Amos pushed his tongue into my mouth. I was shaking so I could hardly stand. Then he pushed me to my knees, pressed my face against his crotch, and . . . .

At this I awoke. How long had I slept? I was shivering in a fetal position in the corner of my bed, my back pressed against the wall. I clutched my pillow which was drenched in sweat. For a moment I though everything — Robbie's death, Abbot Placid's office, these talks with Amos — all was just a dream. What was real then? I looked around.

Outside it was dark. The window rattled as a capricious wind blew gusts of snow against the glass. Most fell back but a few flakes clung desperately before melting. They looked like newly departed souls clammoring to get into heaven. But God didn't exist. If he did, where was he? I heard only wind. I felt nothing but cold. I saw nothing but endless, yawning night.

At that moment I could have beat my hands bloody, not from rage but despair. This darkness was not only an abyss outside my window, it had seeped inside me as well, an aching hunger that gnawed at every cell in my body.

I remembered an apple I'd saved from lunch. Switching on the desk lamp I looked around for it. Ah, there it is next to Kierkegaard's diary. I bit into it as if I'd never eaten before, as if my teeth had never before pierced red skin or chomped into white flesh. At first its juices revived me, then the hunger returned.

I grabbed the Kierkegaard and opened it at random. Meaningless squiggles swirled on the page, a photographic negative of the snow hitting my window. I shut my eyes, breathed deeply a few times, and then, despite a throbbing headache, forced myself to read:

> The rebellion of a crowd triumphs if one cedes the way so that it never comes to realize what it is doing. A crowd has no essential viewpoint; therefore, if it happens to kill a man it is *eo ipso* halted. It pays heed and comes to its sense.

But this was a lie. In matters of sexuality the Church had never come to its senses. If Robbie rose from his coffin and preached a sermon on the subject the Church still wouldn't budge. I hurled the book across the room with such fury that plaster fell from the wall. Amos came running. I glared at him through the small window in the door.

"How can you stay in this wretched place if you have any heart at all," I rasped.

"Would life be any different elsewhere?" He shrugged. "I tried to warn you."

Amos looked like he wanted to say more but he thought better of it and locked the window shutter with a dull click. How that sound rings in my ears now.

Then a more disturbing thought struck me. How was it I was locked up while Theodosius walked free? That very morning I'd seen him strolling across the courtyard. Whatever these monks were they weren't stupid. They must have convinced Sheriff Atkins that I, not Theodosius, had caused Robbie's death. How would they have portrayed it — a lovers' quarrel, the outburst of a crazy person?

Trying vainly to recall Sheriff Atkins' questions, I noticed an old-fashioned air vent behind my cot. A foot and a half square, it was just large enough for me to squeeze through. But how to unscrew the grill? I looked feverishly about — books, writing paper, pen — that was it. The clip of the pen. I broke it off and, as it was too thin to provide leverage, I bent it back and forth till it broke in half. Doubled together, the two pieces fit the screw wedges perfectly. To keep from cutting my fingers I held the edges with my tee shirt as I twisted. Soon the grill was off and I squeezed into the hole, slowly inching forward. More than once I feared getting stuck but when the tunnel turned downward, moving got easier. At last I came to another opening.

Luckily the wood holding the grill screws was rotten enough for me to push it out. It fell with an echoing clank. I followed, landing on hard cement with a painful thud. Where I'd landed was pitch black and cold as the devil's anus. I shivered, feeling my way along damp walls till somewhere ahead I heard voices.

"You fool! Who knows where he's gone. Your orders were to stay with him."

The harsh voice was that of my deadliest enemy. It was soon followed by a wobbly flashlight beam. Had I come this far just to be recaptured? Across from me I felt a draft and followed it into another passageway,

"If he's headed for the exit, we've got him trapped, Luke's there."

"That simpleton? Where are your brains, Amos? We can't let him get away. I want someone dependable covering that exit and the doors into the basilica too."

As they moved down the corridor behind me I breathed easier. It wasn't just their voices that chilled me. Theodosius's bad leg dragged across the floor like a lizard's tail.

When I could no longer hear them, I began inching forward. The passageway was pitch dark and I didn't know where it led. My heart pounded. I stopped and bent over to catch my breath. The air smelled damp, almost as slimey as the walls. I remembered a Hershey in my shirt pocket. I broke off a piece and ate it.

Then, in the distance, I heard another sound — a

faint moaning. It was somewhere ahead of me. As I moved forward I began to make out words. They rose and fell, died out only to recommence like a plaintive Gregorian chant:

> Yesssesus loves ME,
> YES, esus loves me,
> Yes, Jesus loves ME . . .

Luke. He probably felt more frightened down here than I. Despite his gruff appearance, he and Father Raymond were Inviolate's sweetest monks. Their childish minds kept them pure. But would Luke let me escape? I had no choice but to take the risk. When I got close enough I called out.

"Armand, that you?" Luke's quavering voice answered.

"Ya, it's me." Luke turned his flashlight beam from the wall  and into my face.

"Father Theo says you been very bad, Armand. He says you hurt Robbie. Why did you do that? Robbie was my friend. Amos says if I see you I'm supposed to make you go back to your room.

"I didn't hurt Robbie, Luke. Robbie and I were friends too, you know that. And friends don't hurt each other right? Look, I brought you some candy." I held the rest of my Hershey bar out to him.

"Candy, for me?" Luke sounded uncertain. "But Father Theo and Amos said you've been bad. You're supposed to stay in your room."

"Theo and Amos are wrong Luke. I loved Robbie. I . . . I . . ."

Suddenly I couldn't help myself. I started crying. Luke came over and hugged me and began crying himself.

"Whoever hurt Robbie wants to hurt me too Luke," I blurted, recollecting the danger I was in. "Will you help me?"

"But why would anybody hurt you?"

"I don't know, Luke, but I have to get away. And you mustn't tell anybody you saw me, not even Theo or Amos."

"I'll help. You and Robbie are my friends."

Luke unlocked a weathered door and pulled it open, shining his flashlight up the stairs. A parka hung on a hook near the top. I scampered up two steps at a time, grabbed the parka and pushed open the door leading outside. A blast of wind and snow stung my face. I was too happy to care. I could have danced a jig I was so glad to have escaped that cathedral of bestiality. I dragged the parka behind me ten yards before putting it on. Hopefully, the snow would soon cover my remaining tracks.

Before long I reached the highway. My feet burned from snow that had gotten into my shoes. Fortunately, after twenty minutes or so, I was able to flag down a ride.

"Pretty bad night for hitchiking isn't it," said the elderly farmer who'd picked me up.

"You wouldn't believe how bad," I replied. "I've never felt so cold in all my life."

# The World

# One

Hitching back to Milo took three rides and almost thirty-five hours. A smiling woman on a bank billboard urged me to plan for the future. I was. I planned to ask my grandfather, a retired doctor, to lend me money to go Boston, maybe even Europe. Change, a new life — that's what I needed. Grandfather thought otherwise. What I needed most, he argued, was a job.

"All this schooling," he began my second night home. "What's it for? You wanna teach, be a professional? Fine. But I won't support you to be a bum. Work for awhile and you'll appreciate money, get these crazy notions outta your head."

"Like my parents, huh?"

"Your father was a good man, worked hard. Your dreamy, layabout mother was his downfall."

"Now Henry," Grandmother cut in. She was clearing dinner dishes and hated confrontations. Besides, Grandfather was supposed to watch his blood pressure.

"Well it's true, Kate." Grandfather demonstrated his practicality by digging his fork into a large slab of peach pie. When he'd stuffed it into his mouth, he resumed. "If Armand here's so smart, why ain't he rich? It's time he learned to support himself instead of reading books all day."

Then the phone rang. Grandfather answered. It was someone from the monastary.

"I don't know what you're talkin' about," he bellowed. "We haven't seen or heard from him in years. But if he left you folks, I'd say he must be doin' something right."

He slammed down the receiver. Grandfather, a staunch Presbyterian, never approved of my Catholic upbringing in the first place, let alone my decision to enter the monastary. It was just one more example of my mother's baleful influence, an influence he'd done his best to erradicate.

But what if Sheriff Atkins called, or the Milo police?

I looked around the dining room — still tidy as the insides of a Swiss watch — and remembered my first meal here. I was afraid of soiling the tablecloth, of asking which spoon to use for soup. My legs swung nervously under the table. That's how I felt now listening to the cuckoo clock ticking on the wall above Grandfather's head.

Beneath the clock was a cherrywood cabinet on which sat a fifteen gallon fish tank. When I was thirteen I used to spend hours gazing at it, especially at an elephant fish that used to hide in a little rock cave. Every so often it would dart out its snout and worry the angelfish swimming by. Now only the angelfish remained. Maybe it was time I left too. I decided to visit my old friend Trollson.

Trollson, a graduate student in physics, lived in a small hotel near Milo's campus. Slightly deaf, he spoke in a clipped British accent. He was further distinquished by protruding eyes, a photographic memory, and a vivid if unhealthy imagination. We used to take long walks during which he would tell me about Wittgenstein's quarrel with Russell or the history of human torture.

Each step to Trollson's was a meditation upon the disparate elements of my past: my mother and Sister Madeline in New Orleans, being teased for my Southern accent when I first went to school in Milo, my first experience of snow — a beautiful soft blanket spread over every hurt in the world. If only Robbie could be with me now. But what would he make of Trollson or vice versa?

52

I remembered Trollson's first and only date. He'd taken her to watch him at target practice. Afterwards, he'd leaned over and whispered: "Tell me Judy, what would you do if I *shot* you?" That's what my cousin said Judy told him anyway. I had no reason to doubt it.

The second floor hall of Trollson's hotel was darker and mustier than I remembered. I ran my fingers along the peeling, yellowed wallpaper — scenes of Colonial America — until I got to door 23. I knocked. After a few seconds, the door flew open. Trollson jumped out at me like the elephant fish from its cave.

"Dupre!" he exclaimed, as if I'd only been gone a week. "At last I've unravelled the problem of Wild Knots."

If Inviolate had changed me, Trollson took no more notice of it than my grandfather did. For them I was just a passive listener. But after a short lecture on Wild Knots, Trollson agreed to let me sleep on his floor while I looked for a job. Within ten days I found one, a teaching job in Brownsville, some seventy miles away.

Don Burton, whom I'd met in an English class, was now Brownville's Superintendant of Schools. He needed a high school English teacher for the Spring semester. I'd teach history and art on the side. Not only was I desperate for money, I was also curious to see how Burton might function in the buckle of the Bible Belt.

Burton had a gravelly voice, prematurely grey hair, and a girth that almost matched his height of five feet. Capping his self-confidence was a crude, slapstick sense of humor. "How's your weenie?" was one of his favorite expressions. I'd soon discover that he'd become only slightly more sophisticated. I tried to emmulate his authoritarian bluster.

"I'm Armand Dupre of the Iron Axe," I thundered to my first class. I slammed a book down on my desk for emphasis. Twenty-five faces stared up at me in abject terror. I figured it would be best to start strict and loosen up later. In history I assigned extra reading (Eliade and Plato) and in my senior English class I handed out mimeoed copies of Swift's *Modest Proposal.*

"Swift's solution to poverty is perfectly logical," I argued. "Besides, he was a preacher so how could he be wrong?"

Something in me had changed. I wasn't sure what but I could feel it. Maybe Amos was right. What if life *was* the same everywhere? Then I'd have to harden myself. But I couldn't shed my idealism, my yearning for something better. What I wanted my students to discern was the difference between logical and moral solutions. If they could do that, maybe they could better evaluate U.S. policy in Vietnam. But my plan backfired. The next morning before class, Burton stormed through the door.

"What's this you're teachin' the kids about some preacher sayin' we should eat the poor?"

Round and round we went, me in my new herringbone jacket and he with his shirtsleeves rolled. Burton was perspiring and his beer gut spilled over his belt. He pounded my desk. Added to my sins was the fact that I'd been seen reading a paperback of *Tom Jones* as I took tickets for a basketball game the night before. The cover showed an open-shirted boy surrounded by buxom women.

"The parents are up in arms about you, Dupre."

"Stupidity's not a virtue in itself."

"Just let me handle the PR around here!" Burton slapped his fist into a fat palm for emphasis. "From now on just stick to the textbook."

The idea of this pornographic penguin handling PR was ludicrous. A few days earlier he'd shocked the first teacher's meeting I attended by suggesting more intercourse was needed between parents and teachers. But it's not sexual crudity that angers Fundamentalists so much as freedom of thought. Burton thrived because he was willing to sacrifice the latter.

So I stuck to the textbook and, as I'd done so many times before, tried to conform to the behavior expected of me. At 5 p.m., I walked home four blocks from

Brownville's crumbling two-story red brick schoolhouse to my tiny attic apartment in the home of a retired farmer named Smitty. I'd play Bach or Pachelbel as I fixed dinner. Then, sipping scotch and Seven-Up, I'd clear the table and grade papers, or prepare the following week's syllabus which had to be handed into Burton every Friday. Afterwards I'd sink into a faded, stuffed armchair to read. Mostly I read 18th-century novels, imagining myself a deposed duke in exile. Around midnight I'd go to bed.

Alone in the empty double bed how great my suffering became. The images of two students, like temptations to St. Anthony, flickered against the black screen of my closed eyelids. One was an irrepressible tenth grader named Hal who reminded me slightly of Robbie; the other, a slender twelfth grade basketball star named Jim. Hal was more frolicsome and giggled delightedly as I bit his salty neck. Jim's lips were more tremulous as I parted his teeth with my tongue. As they slipped out of their clothes in my dreams, I addicted them to pleasures so intense that something surely must have spilled into their own dreams too, troubling them and leaving them with yearnings for which they knew neither the reason nor the cause.

In one scenario, two padded clamps attached to pulleys and ropes were affixed to Jim's ankles and his hands were tied behind him. As Hal and I divested him of his clothes, cutting and tearing when necessary, Jim would writhe and squirm angrily. When his anger reached truly tendentious proportions, I would yank him into the air. Standing on the bed naked, Hal would then boldly extend his tongue down into Jim's anal garden, sedulously cleaning and pruning it of dingleberries and tufts of hair. While Jim's fingers vainly tried to block and parry these naughty thrusts, I would catch with my mouth whatever other appendages (nipples, lips or cock) poked wildly in my direction.

Once Jim's cock was caught the game was won for

I milked it so fervently, taking care to massage his balls into a tight little package, that any thought but pleasure flew from his addled mind. If by any chance my lips slipped from their duties. Jim would stab and flay the air spasmodically with great spurts and cries as if he were no longer human, but transformed into a great mythic bird in its death throes. Gently I would then lower this shuddering, wondrous creature back onto the bed whereupon I would attempt to revive it with a good hot fucking.

I pictured Hal sitting down in my lap until my cock was embedded deeply within him. As he wrapped his legs tightly around me, I would stand and give him a joyful mid-air fucking. Boys birds, birds boys. Why they flew to me in my dreams this way I don't know. These dreams must have had some astral effect too for the next morning in class, Jim and Hal would stare up at me like hungry, mooing cows.

After three months, however, these chimerical delights no longer sufficed. It wasn't just sex I missed. I ached for intimacy. I'd heard from a monastary friend that Robbie's death had been declared an accident — less scandal than scouring the country for me and having to endure the publicity of a homosexual murder trial. Abbot Placid was so sensible, so diplomatic. Now the monks could appear forgiving for deciding not to prosecute. But what if I returned? What if I insisted on telling the truth? Who'd believe me, the queer offspring of an insane, drunken mother, I thought of killing Theodosius but what would that prove? Only that he was right all along.

These thoughts exausted me and I threw myself into teaching for respite. But this too was a trap. Hal's smiling face increasingly reminded me of Robbie, He'd linger after class to ask questions. I could hardly restrain myself.

Then Spring arrived with thawing snow and the budding of new leaves. But for me the earth was a wound, One afternoon I was walking home in a light drizzle. I wasn't thinking anything, just staring at the sidewalk and watching how high the raindrops bounced and at what angle. A sudden gust of wind jerked my left arm so violently that the umbrella I was carrying snapped down over my head.

At this I felt exactly as I had when Amos first hugged me — as if the earth had suddenly swallowed me — and I began to laugh, I couldn't stop. I felt as if the extreme depth but impossible stupidity of my life had been snuffed out.

"Are you okay, Mr. Dupre?"

I thought it was Robbie's voice for an instant but when I got the umbrella off my head I saw Jim staring at me from the open window of his red Chevy. Two other students peered at me from inside.

"Just this damn umbrella," I laughed. I was grateful that the rain disguised the tears streaming down my cheeks.

"Can we give you a lift?"

How long had they been watching me? I wasn't sure. I accepted Jim's offer and, when I got home, went straight to bed. Almost immediately I fell asleep and began to dream.

Robbie appears looking confused. I'm surprised to see him but grateful too. We're late to a party at Mrs. Zurfis's. When we arrive I knock but no one answers. Finally the door opens and a fat, friendly man greets us with open arms. I see Mrs. Zurfis over his shoulder, her arms folded over a green quilted robe.

"This is my husband Jack," she says. "I've told you about him, remember?"

Jack throws his arms over our shoulders and leads us to a crackling fire. Lines radiate from his eyes like sun rays drawn by a child. "Well don't just stand there, have some brandy," he laughs. Mrs. Zurfis comes in with a pot of steaming coffee. Plates full of cookies, stuffed dates, cheese and crackers and a bowl of candy kisses are already on the table. Robbie hugs everyone and dances with Mrs. Zurfis. The room swirls with gossip and laughter. Gradually, the other seminarians begin to leave. Only Robbie and I remain.

"Fix the guest room for the boys," Jack says. Something about his cheerfulness bothers me.

Mrs. Zurfis scurries upstairs. I follow to see if there's anything I can do. When I enter the guestroom she snatches my hand and squeezes it tightly.

"Look at the sheets," she whispers. Before I can ask what she means, she's gone.

Puzzling over her behavior, I look around. Red high school pennants are tacked over a flowered brown and rose wallpaper. A thick quilt of concentric squares — burgundy, brown, green, orange, red, gold — covers the double bed. How good it feels to be with Robbie in a friendly home at last. I pull back the quilt. The sheets are smeared with blood.

This dream feels more real than my life.

The next few weeks were uneventful. Some students learned, others didn't. Aside from one parent's complaint that I suggested that their son read Updike's *Rabbit Run*, I managed to keep Don Burton off my back. But I grew bored. A snowy winter and rainy spring cooped me up in Smitty's attic, which was far lonelier than even my monastary cell. Then I read a *Time* article about hippies. "LSD expands your mind so that you feel at one with the whole universe," one kid said. Maybe that's what I needed. The next weekend I drove back to Milo to see if I could find this new drug.

"Got no acid but I got some Speed," Chris said. Ten tiny pills fell into my hand — five red and five yellow.

"And this is like LSD?"

"Sorta."

Chris shrugged as he stuffed my five dollars into his pocket. He was a handsome art student whose James Dean demeanor made him seem more sincere, if not stable, than most of my Milo cronies. At least he'd never lied to me yet. "It makes you feel kinda groovy. I like to read and paint on it."

I wasn't sure what Speed was but the following Friday evening I began to eat them as I read Iris Murdoch's *A Severed Head*. Nothing seemed to happen so half an hour later I ate more. After seven I began to feel a loving loquacious glow. If only Hal and Jim were with me now, my seeds of fantasy might finally bloom; but getting up for the bathroom, I collapsed. I was on fire, then freezing. If I moved so much as a little finger my heartbeat doubled. By the time I inched my way to the stairwell the next morning I felt my heart was ready to burst.

"I had a bad reaction to some medicine," I called down to Smitty. "Can you get some tranquilizers from Dr. Varnes?"

I was sure I'd soon die — this time for real. Smitty must have thought so too. When he hobbled up to see what ailed me, he dashed back downstairs as if he'd come in contact with a ghost. Valium saved me, but for the next several days I was too weak to get out of bed.

Under the white chenille bedspread I lay still as a corpse. At the foot of the bed was a heavy dresser with an oval mirror. Propped up on two fluffy pillows, I could see outside the window by its reflection. At last the sun was shining. There was no tree or bush to cast a shadow. Smitty knocked on my door announcing visitors and, before I knew it, Hal and Jim stood by my bed. Hal's lips were red as gardenias against his cream-white skin. Jim's browner skin looked soft as an eraser.

"You're lookin' awful pale, Mr. Dupre," Jim drawled. "You gonna be okay?"

"Sure. Just a bad reaction to some medicine."

"We sure miss you," Hal piped cheerfully. "Miss Stovall's a *lousy* substitute."

I wanted to tell them that if they each kissed me, maybe then I'd return to health, but even this thought agitated my overwrought heart. I pictured St. Catherine of Siena sucking the wounds of plague victims. But it wasn't my heart that needed sucking nor was it their kind hearts that excited my amorous propensities. "The charms of heaven in the bush are superceded, I fear, by heaven in the hand," as Emily Dickinson once observed.

Outside a cloud passed the window and the mirror darkened to the color of slate. Not knowing what to do with his hands, Jim thrust them into the back pockets of his jeans, Nervously he shuffled his feet. First he looked at the ceiling, then at the floor. Hal stared at a stack of books on the chair next to my bed. If anything more exciting had happened I'd certainly tell you — from the cracks of the floor maybe, or from the bed.

"Well, guess we gotta be goin,'" Jim said at last.

"I'll be okay, don't worry." I smiled weakly. "Nice of you to drop by."

Once again I'd overcome temptation but this didn't soothe my tortured soul. Increasingly I had to fight off these rapacious dream boys, these birds of my imagination.

When my contract expired that June, the good parents of Brownsville were no doubt as relieved to see me go as I was to be leaving. But I'd accomplished my goal. I'd saved enough money to go to Europe.

# Two

Paris!

I shall always know it by the name Tomaso, for on that night of June 24th, Feast of John the Baptist, when I flew in amidst the glittering array of lights strung across the city like pearls, what was revealed with a dramatic instance was not the Eiffel Tower, Notre Dame or any other diadem splendor, but the eerie illumination of his soul calling "Armand, Armand," even before we met.

He was twenty-four, an actor, the youngest son of a wealthy Italian manufacturer. He was bored with life and not even the coke piled high on silver platters, the nights of hustling in Montmartre dives, or the films he'd recently appeared in to growing critical acclaim had been enough to quench his thirst for meaning.

"You think I like wearing dark glasses so no one will know me? You think I like those yachting parties with Queen this and Contessa that?"

His black eyes flashed, overwhelming every other feature of his classic face. Classic? His nose wasn't quite strong enough to be Roman but turned up slightly at the end. His eyebrows, when furrowed, slid downward like kids on a sled. His face was plastic and could assume any form. No wonder he was such a good actor. He could appear comic, grotesque, evil or innocent yet each face was equally seductive. "Cold, imperious, deep," critics called him in his last film, but this was not the face he turned to me now. He looked like a tiny, frightened baby rabbit. I sloshed Dubonnet in my glass as if the obsessive circular motion might draw us back together.

"Why don't you give it all up then?"

"It's not that easy."

Biting his lower lip, he turned to the balcony. Tourists emptied from a bus below us and flooded across the square to throw coins in an ornate fountain. A majestic statue twisted its massive bronze muscles as if to emerge from the night into a golden spotlight. A year ago this scene might have impressed me.

"*Abbiamo davanti a noi i corni di un dilemma*," Tomaso muttered.

Yes, we sat on the horns of a dilemma.


I'd met him while selling pen and ink sketches of Notre Dame on St. Germain. Eva, my vivacious Swedish friend, was helping me by grabbing passers-by and gushing, "Oh, don't you think this one's marvelous?" When she grabbed Tomaso's arm, he laughed.

"Everybody's got a racket, don't they?"

But then he looked at the drawings and liked them. Taken by our zaniness, he offered to buy one if we'd join him for a drink.

I'd met Eva just two weeks earlier. I was waiting in line for opera tickets with Bill Speer, a history prof who was another of my Milo mentors. He did research at the Bibliothèque Nationale every summer, and I used to grade papers for him.

"Dare ya to ask her for a date," Bill taunted when he saw me staring at her. She was standing alone looking up at a fresco. Her blond hair was tucked up under a blue Maoist cap and she hugged a baggy leather jacket tightly around her waist.

"I don't know . . ." My desire to be thought virile waged a little war with my shyness.

"Oh, go on," Bill urged. His prompting tipped the scales. I took a deep breath and approached her.

"*Excusez-moi*, I've just come to Paris and I'm feeling kinda lonely. You look interesting so I was, uh, wondering if I might take you to dinner."

Eva smiled. Up close she looked even more stunning: creamy complexion, plump cheeks, rosy cherubic lips . . . .

"That would be very nice," she said simply. After chatting a while we made plans to meet on the Opera House steps the next evening.

Inside I glowed. I'd never asked a beautiful girl for a date before. Would she kiss me? But what if she changed her mind and didn't show up? I tried to ignore my nervousness the next day by drawing. I'd brought a sketchbook to Paris because I'd heard that the French respect artists more than Americans do. If someone came over to look at my sketches, I could take out a cigarette" say *"Avez-vous du feu?"* and start a conversation. But Eva I'd met on my own.

Despite my fears, she showed up as planned wearing the same black leather jacket over a blue knit dress. Her blond hair was tied, Kamakazi style, with a red silk scarf. I wore my usual — jeans, tennis shoes, and my gray herringbone sportcoat. We found a tiny Algerian restaurant in the Latin Quarter and sat at a table next to the wall.

"I've only been here a few days myself," Eva began, "I'm very lucky you asked me to dinner because I'm — how do you say — broken."

"Broke, you mean?"

"That's right, broke!" Eva laughed. "You must help me with my English. Anyway, I just wonder what to do when I met you. My father wires me money but it hasn't come yet."

Eva's trouble with English pleased me. If she didn't know a word in English, she'd say it in French and I'd look it up in my red plastic pocket dictionary. Eva'd been a dancer in the Stockholm ballet, she said, but had broken her legs in a boating accident. Now she taught dance to children and designed clothes.

"I'm a teacher too," I said. "But this summer I just

want to draw."

I showed her my sketchpad. Her enthusiasm was contagious. Indeed, she delighted in everything. We started to hang out so much together that people mistook us for lovers.

"So where shall we go?" Tomaso laughed, caught up in our giddy mood, His face was shiny with happiness and, despite his expensive white sweater, he bounced down the street like a guttersnipe. I suggested a cafe near my hotel. If I shut my eyes I can still picture its mirror behind the bar, the little marble table where we sat, the bright yellow lights which flooded out onto the sidewalk. But how to describe my first impression of Tomaso? He was slender but well built, his features softer than the Marlboro man's yet more distinctive than an *Esquire* model's. Dark Medusa curls fell to his collar and he had a mole beneath his left ear. But it was especially his eyes — mischievous and dangerous — that riveted me. They seemed to mock me and say "We know what you want even more than you do."

First he was a vacationing schoolboy. He'd studied at Cambridge, he said. Then he was a schoolboy pretending to be an artist. He claimed to have met Dali and Picasso, who'd encouraged him to paint. His stories kept changing. Did he really like us or was he just putting us on? I felt my desire rise, fall, then rise again, a hapless buoy in the rippling sea of his being, He tied the arms of his sweater around his neck and, interlocking his fingers, stretched his arms up over his head and cracked his knuckles. When he noticed that I was gazing at him even more intently than Eva did, he told us of a blind old Austrian he'd met who used to be lovers with Prince Edward at Cambridge. Nazis had put out the man's eyes in the war. Now he lived on a pension in Paris. Tomaso was helping him put up some shelves but the old guy kept chasing him around the apartment. What should he do? I pretended disinterest offering pedestrian advice.

Eva was sure she'd seen Tomaso someplace. He

said no, he didn't think so. When he left to use the rest-room, she remembered.

"Wasn't your picture in *Le Soir* recently?" she asked when he returned.

"Ya, I'm Danny the Red, the student anarchist," he laughed. "I just dyed my hair today so the cops wouldn't catch me."

"No, I'm serious," Eva pressed. "Turn your head sideways."

"Like this?"

He straightened his back, turned his head right, and smoothing his hair back with the fingers of his left hand, slowly raised his chin. For an instant, he was Garbo.

"Or would you prefer this?"

He turned towards me now, lowered his eyes slightly, and furrowed his brow with the alert intensity of Jean-Pierre Léaud. Then he tossed his head back, inhaled from a Sobranie, and exhaling, grinned at me like Dionysius. His lips curled like waves. My eyes became seagulls. I wanted to dive into him.

"Okay," he said, turning to Eva again. "I'm Tomaso Bianchi, the 'rising star.' I didn't want to tell you before because — well, since you didn't recognize me, I wondered what it would feel like to be treated like an ordinary guy."

"But why should it matter if you're a movie star or not?"

"It shouldn't but it always seems to," Tomaso sighed. "Anyway, thanks for the company. I really enjoyed it, Gotta go now, have an early shoot tomorrow."

"Would you join us for dinner later this week?" Tomaso's eyes brightened at my suggestion. He looked at Eva.

"Please do. We've had fun too."

"Friday okay? Say we meet here at eight?"

"Great," I replied. Tomaso slapped me on the shoulder and pecked Eva on each cheek as he left. I looked at his half-finished drink, the butts of his black and gold cigarettes in the ashtray, a doodle he'd scrawled on a napkin. I picked up one of his Sobranie's and slipped it into my shirt pocket. When I got back to my room I smoked it. Would Tomaso's lips taste as rich or sweet?

Our Friday dinner went well. Tomaso was still flirtatious but less mocking than before. Or had I been paranoid? Actors, after all, are notoriously insecure. Whenever my doubts arose, Tomaso would do or say something to charm me. I marveled at how emotions played over his face. Mine was as impassive as a sphinx.

Eva and I, meanwhile, had frequent late dinners with Bill. He was a Reformation scholar with thin sandy hair and a handsome though slightly pockmarked jaw. His research focused on the sect of Free Spirits John Calvin had condemned as libertines. Bill saw the hippies as parallel. Although only seven years older than I, Bill had lived in Paris previously and enjoyed guiding me and Eva around. We told him about Tomaso and he suggested we all have dinner together which we soon did.

Bill didn't care much for Tomaso but seemed amused at the dynamics of our circle. Perhaps he was jealous of the actor. His urbane cynicism sharpened when Tomaso was with us.

"There's Les Deux Magots where Sartre and De Beauvoir used to sit. I see Simone in the Bibliothèque Nationale a lot, a tragic figure who wears orange stockings and a dowdy navy-blue dress with white polka dots. She looks like a lonely old whore."

"Better a lonely old whore than a lonely old maid," Tomaso replied.

"I suppose you're an expert?"

"'Man is more prone to vengeance than to gratefulness. Favors are writ in dust but stripes we feel. Depraved nature stamps in lasting steel.'" Tomaso arched his brow and smiled. "That's the Jacobean playwright John Marston."

Bill's face reddened. Not only had his marriage

failed, he was seething with bitterness over the red tape of trying to get an annulment, leaving the Church he considered unthinkable. He was hot for Eva but, like everyone, assumed she and I were lovers, Bill's misunderstanding was fine with Eva and did my ego no harm either.

"I'm glad to see *someone*'s erudite!" Bill puffed on his pipe, his lips thinner than before.

Tomaso quickly moved to assuage Bill's feelings. In fact, he became so solicitous, so intrigued by Bill's research, that Bill soon found himself as charmed by Tomaso as Eva and I had been. So our leisurely dinner threesomes became foursomes. We attended Ionesco's *The Bald Soprano* together and then, Bergman's *Persona*.

I wanted to fuse into Tomaso as the two women had at the end of the movie but Tomaso ran ahead to tell Eva of some new bistro he'd discovered. Tonight he was the mischievous child. I meandered behind with Bill who played bon vivant even as he carried all the suffering of the world on his shoulders. "My Cross," as he fondly put it.

Odors of lamb shish-ka-bob wafted from Algerian restaurants, prostitutes beckoned from doorways, unkempt hippies — some from wealthy Parisian families — pestered us for change. I tried to imagine the look of this narrow Left Bank street in the fourteenth century: gargantuan shop signs creaking in the wind, street vendors and students shouting, the clatter of horse's hooves over — but cobblestones weren't invented yet. Only mud and manure sloped down into an evil-smelling drainage ditch in the middle of the road.

A bell in the distance reminded me of public criers solemnly announcing deaths: "Wake you sleepers, pray God forgive your trespasses. The dead cannot cry. Pray for their souls as the bell sounds in these streets." I was learning to be tough but church bells broke me down. Somewhere a stray dog howled. Bill announced that he'd decided to turn in early.

"Tomaso knows a great place where we can go dancing."

Eva threw her arm around my waist and nuzzled my shoulder. I consented, eager to shake the gloom Bill and the Bergman film had cast over me. Tomaso's eyes sparkled as he led us through increasingly steep streets to Montmartre and finally up a dark alley. A swarthy, hulking man, whose sleeveless tee shirt revealed tattooed snakes curling down his biceps to his wrist, took our money at the door.

Inside a dingy lamp hung precariously over the bar. A few candles stuck in wine bottles offered the only other light. Sweaty bodies gyrated to loud recorded music, mostly Soul, amidst cigarette smoke thick as fog. We ordered drinks. Tomaso took a tiny bottle from his pocket that was filled with blue grey powder. He unscrewed the cap, dipped in a tiny silver spoon, held it up to his right nostril and snorted.

"What's that?"

"MDA, want some?" He repeated the operation with his left nostril.

"Sure, why not." I tried to sound nonchalant. Whatever Tomaso did, I wanted to do. He represented a new life, everything I wanted. For once I felt I fit in.

After snorting some of Tomaso's powder, I looked back at the dance floor. Aretha Franklin's "Train, Train, Train" had just come on and sparks flew up from the dancer's heels. I danced with Eva, then Tomaso did. Eva's breasts bounced playfully as she leapt around in a circle (a prancing fawn). Tomaso undulated his hips slowly in a circular movement that started in his knees and wound up his body until his fingers snapped over his head like a whip (a Morrocan lion tamer).

Two lithe girls whirled deliriously. Then I noticed one was a boy. Off the dance floor he seemed timid, almost invisible, but dancing he transfixed me. He leapt in the air. Were he and the girl lovers or was their lovemaking all in the dance?

Two muscular young men had fastened their belts together. Their jeans were unzipped revealing red nylon bathing suits. Their smooth, naked torsos glistened with sweat as they rubbed together in time to the music. Whistles screeched through the air. Waves of feeling rushed up and down my spine. Everything began to melt, to merge before my eyes.

"Come on," Eva laughed, pulling me up from the table and onto the floor. I shut my eyes and let the music carry me. Sly and The Family Stone began to take me higher, Then I fell into Mick Jagger's plaintive moan in "Wild Horses." Eva's body was soft and white, Tomaso's tan and hard. Our arms entwined, wove around each other's shoulders like threads in a carpet. Wild horses couldn't drag me away. But when the song ended, Tomaso did. We returned to our table.

Tomaso's white shirt was now unbuttoned to his waist. His bronze chest glistened as if he'd just stepped out of a swimming pool. He shook sweat out of his hair like a dog and dropped into the chair next to me, squeezing the nape of my neck. He smelled like everything I ever wanted.

"Bet you never been to a place like this before."

I could feel his body heat pulsating towards me. I wanted to lean over, kiss him. I leaned over. He pushed me away.

"Look at Eva, not me!"

"But *you're* the movie star," Eva giggled. "Who are we supposed to look at if not you?"

"Okay," Tomaso laughed, raising his hands in surrender. "But it's time to leave. I have to work in the morning.

We stumbled outside. Cold air stabbed my muscles. Tomaso hailed a cab and pushed me in first so that Eva sat between us. I felt confused, angry. The cab lurched roughly over the cobblestones and turned a sharp right. Eva and Tomaso slid over, crushing me against the door.

I didn't fit anymore.

The next morning Eva called me for breakfast. I was surprised to find Tomaso with her when I arrived at the cafe.

"My shoot was postponed for two days," he said cheerfully. Even in jeans and a tee shirt he looked flawless. I hated him for it. I hated him even more when he said, "You sure were loaded last night. How'd you get the name Armand anyway? I thought American guys were always named Bill, or Joe."

"No, some are named Benedict or Arnold," I replied tartly. "And some with snobbish backgrounds are named *Lance*."

Despite my hangover and irritation, I still wanted him. I wanted to hit him and wipe that arrogant smirk off his face. I was tired of being good. Tomaso asked if we'd like to hitch to Chartres with him.

"I've got to see a clothes buyer this afternoon," Eva said. "But you guys go on. And be sure to do some sketches for me, Armi, okay?"

I had nothing better to do so I agreed.

Once outside the city, the charm of the French countryside took hold. At first I didn't say much and Tomaso didn't either. Then he began chatting in French to the driver, a middle aged carpenter who'd picked us up in his truck. They spoke too rapidly for me to follow. Twenty miles outside Paris, the carpenter let us out.

The road was hot and dusty. Tomaso said the driver suggested we shortcut through the field to a road where we could get rides easier. After twenty minutes, we saw some peasants stacking hay with pitchforks. They looked like they were posing for postcards. In the distance I could hear some birds but didn't know what kind.

"Probably robins or thrushes," Tomaso said.

He seemed content to walk in silence. I couldn't tell what he was feeling behind his dark glasses. When we got near the highway, he grabbed my arm and pointed to the sky. A hawk soared up from a clump of trees. I looked back at Tomaso. He was smiling. I smiled back. For once we were on an equal footing and I was glad I'd come. If I suffered from the heat, tired leg muscles, or cockleburrs in my shoes, so did he.

When we got to the road a stocky farmer gave us a lift in his ancient Renault, the doors of which rattled as if about to fall off.

The man couldn't understand my French and Tomaso had to restate everything I said. They mocked and exaggerated my accent but I didn't care. In becoming my impertinent protector, I felt Tomaso's attachment to me deepen.

We got to Chartres about three in the afternoon. The Cathedral's magnificent rose window — which cast brilliant petals of yellow, blue and ruby light on the stone floor inside — didn't thrill me as much as our simple picnic on the lawn. We ate bread and camembert cheese under the shade of a poplar. We swigged red wine from a bottle. Tomaso napped while I sketched. At about three we headed back, stopping off to rest at Versailles.

We walked to the rear of the palace and sat down on the steps overlooking the pool. I'd been here before with Bill so I had no interest to explore further. Tomaso lay back and unbuttoned his shirt to take in the remaining sun. His brown nipples were hard and surrounded by sunbleached down. Burial mounds of feeling? An erratic breeze teased my nostrils with the smell of honeysuckle.

"You don't know what you'd be getting yourself in for," Tomaso said as he caught me looking at him. Embarrassed, I looked away. To hide my nervousness, and hoping perhaps to seduce him with my eloquence, I began talking about Robbie. Tomaso cupped his hands behind his head and listened. When I finished, he said, "Ever read *Les Liaisons Dangereuses*?

"No, why?"

"You should." He paused before continuing. "You see, I'm unfortunately not like your Robbie. I'm constitutionally unable to love anyone."

71

He looked at me coldly, undramatically. He said he was born unbearably rich and would destroy anyone who got too close to him. For the rest of our trip he remained aloof.

The next day I poured out my heart to Eva in the cafe. What was with Tomaso anyway? Sometimes he was friendly, even blatantly flirtatious, then he'd freeze and back off. What was so terrible about sex anyway? Wasn't Paris supposed to be the city of love?

"Sometimes people like each other better when they don't sleep together."

"Like you and I maybe?"

I stabbed at the butter as if it were an enemy, the source of all misery. The cold, slippery butter fell off my bread.

"There's something I haven't told you," Eva said, stroking the side of her cappuccino cup with her finger. A man wearing horn-rimmed glasses and a beret looked up from his newspaper. He looked down again when I glared at him.

"It's about why I came here," Eva paused again. I crossed my legs nervously vibrating my right foot in the air. Robbie said I used to do it when I slept. Thumper, he called me.

"I was involved with a married man in Stockholm, a lawyer. We met at a party and became friends, like you and I." Eva smiled as she looked at me. "Then Bjorn wanted to sleep with me. Why not, I thought." Eva picked up her cup and carefully wiped coffee off her saucer with a napkin. She folded the napkin placing it between her saucer and cup.

"Why not add sex to our friendship," Eva continued. "Bjorn said he loved me and gradually I fell in love with him. But he wouldn't divorce his wife. He said he would but he didn't." Eva reached over for my napkin.

"So I came here. How else could I forget?" Eva paused still again. I assumed she was finished. "I couldn't stop loving him and . . ."

72

"And I'm not married but I'm queer — that's why you won't sleep with me, right? I'm just a dumb hick from Iowa who nobody wants. Not you, not Tomaso, not anybody."

"Not true," Eva protested. "Don't say that. Maybe Tomaso really is afraid of hurting you."

Eva said she knew something of the social set he travelled in. Rich, bored people were notorious for playing cruel games with each other. It kept their lives interesting. Maybe Tomaso had been hurt himself.

"Oh great," I exploded. "Everyone but me's been too hurt to love. But I'm such a nice, sweet guy I should live under glass, an exemplar of Medieval Romance."

I noticed Eva had a knack for balancing her butter on her croissant till she got it into her mouth. Why could everyone handle life and love but me? Eva said I should relax and enjoy friendship. If I did, sex would surely follow when the right time came. I said I wished people would stop worrying whether I might get hurt and let me take my own risks.

When we left the cafe, Eva was quiet and moody; I had a flat taste in my mouth. I hadn't gotten the sympathy and advice I'd wanted but then neither had she. I felt so sick of being taken for granted that I wanted to scream but screaming wasn't in my nature. I was too inhibited. Maybe I should drink more, or do drugs like Tomaso. Maybe that would loosen me up.

Over the next several days I pressed Tomaso to show me something of the corrupt world he travelled in. At first he teased me about it, then he said he'd consider it, at last he agreed. A bash was being thrown for Pasolini outside Paris. If we wanted to go, he'd take Eva and me along.

My heart pounded in anticipation for the next week. Would Sartre be there or Barthes? I tried to find one of Pasolini's novels or some of his poems in English. All I could find was one of his novels in French. Even with my pocket dictionary it was slow going. Bill told me all the

Pasolini gossip he'd heard, how he was fired from teaching for seducing boys and eloped to Rome with his mother. "He's pretty wild," Bill teased. "I'd watch out if I were you." Bill pretended he was too busy for such nonsense but I sensed he was hurt that Tomaso hadn't invited him too.

Before I knew it, Saturday arrived. Tomaso picked us up in front of Eva's hotel in a black limousine. The ride was cloud smooth. We smoked some grass but Tomaso refused to give me any of his powder. I was still too green, he said. Then the limo pulled off the highway and, after winding along a country road several miles, entered a white stone gate. A double row of tall, dark shrubs — or were they pines — obscured our view.

Then I saw it, a four-story eighteenth century mansion lit up by floodlights. My expectations for sheer opulence weren't disappointed. Against the night it looked like an enchanted castle.

"It looks like the chateau in *Last Year At Marienbad*!"

"It is," Tomaso laughed. "In fact I was in that flick, my second. Dreadful standing for hours like a statue though."

We joined a string of Mercedes rolling slowly up to a spatulating marble staircase. I counted twenty limos, at least, arching along the gravel drive. When we stopped at the foot of the stairs, a young man in a short ponytail and red silk livery opened our door. To think I'd come from a monastery to this, and in just six months.

"Gotta make my rounds," Tomaso said after we'd climbed the stairs and gone inside. He blew us a kiss. His body, Donatello's *David* alive. "If I meet anyone exciting, I'll come get you."

Tomaso bounded up the winding staircase in the foyer as if he knew his way around. I soon lost sight of him in the crowd. Butlers extended arms to take unnecessary wraps; Women fanned themselves as they exchanged greetings; Elderly gentlemen, some with bandoliers across their chests, stood stiffly next to their wives. Some bowed to kiss white elbow-length gloves. Diamonds sparkled on women's wrists and arms. A crystal chandelier, half as big as my grandparent's dining room table, hung from the twenty foot ceiling. Somewhere a string quartet was playing Mozart.

"Rather stuffy, isn't it." Eva fondled a fern on a black marble table. "See why Tomaso prefers our life on the Left Bank?"

Eva looked ravishing. Tomaso had bought her a black chiffon Dior and loaned her a stone to go with it. Her creamy skin and vibrant face rose up from the smokey gown like a genie from a bottle. Her blond hair was in a French roll but ringlets fell from each side of her face, two tiny waterfalls. The simple onyx hanging from her throat centered her beauty with a hint of deep eroticism. She was too beautiful to need make-up and wore none.

I marveled too at my own reflection in a gold-veined, wall-length mirror behind her. Since meeting Eva and Tomaso, I'd become aware of my own sexiness. I looked as suave and debonair in the tux Tomaso loaned me as any other young aristocrat. Indeed, I looked like Tomaso. More than once, to my delight, I was mistaken for him.

As we moved into the ballroom, waiters offered trays of caviar and champagne. After a few glasses, I began to feel the confidence of my appearance. I looked around for the rock stars and movie actors Tomaso had promised but saw none, at least none that I recognized. Conversations in French and Italian predominated but I heard some English.

"Do you like my calf in these stockings?" A white-haired gentleman was speaking to a boy of about sixteen. "This calf's been a reveller in this house for twenty years. Why I could have carried a lady, or a stable boy too, up those stairs at a trot. And there were some who tried the strength of a man's back."

Eva snickered as I pantomimed the lord by pulling up my pant leg and preening. Who else could I mock or dazzle? On our left, a matron was sharing a recipe:

"You mix thirty-seven yolks of Barbarie hen's eggs, one ounce of Ethiopian dates sweetened with three quarters of a pound of pure candied Indian eringos . . ."

She was interrupted by a younger woman with upswept black hair. The new arrival appeared to have been poured into her black velvet bodice.

"*Je suis certaine que j'ai vecu une autre vie en Espagne. Oui, je l'ai senti à Madrid que j'étais une religiouse cloitrée. En Inde? Comme c'etait pathétique. Mais j'ai acheté une belle tanka en Népal et quand j'ai du temps, je prierai devant elle. Je suis certaine que j'étais bouddhiste une fois, aussi . . .*"

"Buddhist indeed," Eva said as we moved out onto the balcony. Even outside the heat was oppressive. Before I could ask what the woman had said, a long haired kid came up and asked something in slangy French. He was the first person I'd seen with the sense to unbutton his shirt. Maybe he was one of Pasolini's hustlers. When I didn't reply, he mimicked toking on a joint. "*Je le regret,*" I shrugged. He scowled, slapped his bicep in insult, and moved on.

"So this is the world you want to mix in," Eva laughed. "Parties with Lord Auch and Lady Ashe."

I didn't reply. My eyes were frozen on a boy leaning on a balustrade not twenty feet away. I hadn't noticed him before as he'd been looking the other way but when he turned, shaking his mane of blond hair, I dropped my glass. *It was Robbie!*

"What's wrong?" Eva asked urgently. Then I heard Tomaso's voice behind me, distant and muffled as if coming from inside a bottle.

"Not only can I introduce you to Pasolini but guess who he's with — Gore Vidal!" Noticing my stricken face, he followed my gaze. "Ah, so that's it!"

"It's Robbie," I mumbled dumbly. "It can't be but it *is*. It's . . ."

When I came to I didn't know where I was. Then I remembered. My stomach had jumped into my mouth. Then my knees felt weak and I had trouble breathing. Finally, I felt a dizzy panic and everything went black. Now Eva was standing over me sponging my forehead with a cloth soaked in cold eau-de-cologne. I still felt nauseous.

"He did it just to embarrass me," Tomaso hissed, pacing back and forth, "I've heard of knockout beauty before but . . ."

"He just drank his champagne too fast," Eva explained. "It could have happened to anyone. What he needs now is air."

Eva and Tomaso picked me up under each arm and carried me over to a window. A gust of air brought me to. Wrought iron lamps dotted the stairway and drive below. White mink stoles disappeared into black limousines. I took a deep breath. Not only the shock of seeing Robbie but the intensity of Tomaso's anger had overloaded my emotional circuits. Who *did* I love? What was love to carry me to this?

"That wasn't Robbie," Tomaso said coldly. "It was Mick Taylor, the Stone's new guitarist. And, in case you're wondering, he's straight."

Why couldn't Tomaso just shut up. I tried to remember. How could it be — not only the same face, the same features, but the same gestures too — the way he moved his head. I shut my eyes. All I could see was Robbie. Perhaps the guy's hair was a bit longer and he was standing at a distance but . . .

"What I'd *like* to do is throw him out the window," Tomaso said.

"But what you're going to do is take him back to your hotel," Eva retorted. Tomaso stared at Eva in disbelief. Before he could answer, she continued. "Well, we can't take him back to his hotel like this. His last two flights are up a ladder. And we can't leave him here."

I don't recall the ride back except that they stopped

once to let me lean out of the car. Then I was in Tomaso's hotel, far more lavish than mine and with too much light in the lobby. Tomaso had my arm over his shoulder and his arm around my waist. We got into the elevator, down a blue carpeted hall, and into his room. He dropped me on his bed, the biggest I'd ever seen, and began peeling off my clothes. Then he carried me into the shower. I jumped when the cold water hit.

"You shit," I cried out. "Don't you have any feelings at all?"

I started hitting him, he hit back. Only he hit harder. In fact, he exploded.

"This is what you wanted, isn't it? To humiliate me in public, to ruin my career! Well you've probably succeeded. I'm sure the gossip columns tomorrow will be just full of your little scene." With each new accusation, Tomaso slapped me. "You probably like this don't you, you little bitch." He slapped me harder.

"I give up," I cried, sinking down onto the ornate tile floor. "You win."

"Not yet," he replied, grabbing me by the arm. He dragged me from the bathroom back to his bed and threw me down on my stomach. Cold water and the pain of his blows had sobered me up. Looking over my shoulder, I saw him stepping out of his pants. His hairy legs stood in sharp contrast to his smooth bronze chest and arms. His red cock stuck out like a soldering iron at midpoint where god and monster fused.

"Please, Tomaso," I begged. "Not like this."

"You've been wanting to get fucked, haven't you?"

He climbed onto the bed, straddled my legs and lubricated his cock. When he entered me I felt a pain so intense that it transported me into another dimension.

"Stop!" I screamed, but Tomaso only plunged deeper. I tried to squirm away, to fight him off, but he gripped me under my arms and behind my neck in a hammerlock.

"Is this how you used to fuck Robbie?"

At these words the searing pain I felt shifted, not to

pleasure exactly but into something eerily similar — a keen desire to please him. If he insisted on fucking me, I might as well give him the most intense physical pleasure of his life. I wanted to give myself, to exist only for that, to lose myself in his arms. Is this how Robbie had felt with me? I felt I was giving myself to Robbie too, or more exactly, becoming one with him.

What we did now transcended anger. I lifted my buttocks up to meet Tomaso's thrusts. I felt his hot, panting breath on my neck, the power of his need, the sound of his sweaty body and balls slapping against me. I turned my head sideways and our mouths fused in desperate kisses. Our tongues entwined like serpents. I felt caught up in some energy beyond me, something raw at the core of my life, some ancient rhythm or out-of-body experience I'd never before felt.

When Tomaso came he let out a cry that trailed into a moan. Then he fell back exhausted. We both were. I felt a tingling up and down my spine and half wished he was still inside me though greatly relieved that he was not. Then something very strange happened. Tomaso started to cry. I was too tired to move or speak but I'll never forget falling asleep to the anguished but almost silent sound of Tomaso's weeping.

Morning. I awoke with a hangover, feeling sheepish and confused, unclear about what had happened the night before. Suave and debonair indeed! Tomaso was right. I was still green, a small town kid who could only make a fool of myself in his world.

I looked around — crystal chandeliers, glass tables, white carpeting an inch thick, white and gold Louis XIV chairs. I didn't belong here. I could never fit into this world and didn't want to. My tiny four by eight garret in L'Hôtel Monsieur Le Prince suited me fine. So what if I had to climb five flights of stairs, then carry a bucket of water up two more ladders if I wanted to wash my face. Bill said Rimbaud had lived in my hotel, maybe even in my room. That was better than all Tomaso's luxury. In my spartan five franc a night garret I had everything I wanted — books, knapsack, sketch pad.

I looked about for my clothes. Then an absurdity struck me. Here I was in Tomaso's bed at last and I couldn't wait to get out of it. I felt like Rimbaud in the elegant parlor of the Verlaines. I wanted to wreck this place but I was its prisoner. Tomaso wasn't here and I couldn't find my clothes. No sooner did I think this but the door flew open and there he was, all cheer and smiles.

"We're saved," he exclaimed. "There's not a word about us in the papers. My agent must have intervened. Remind me to give him a bonus."

He walked to the window and threw open the shutters, letting harsh sunlight pour in, Then he came over to the bed and plopped down.

"So what do you want for breakfast? I'll ring room service."

My head throbbed, my ass still hurt and I resented his intrusive cheeriness. I resented having to say anything at all.

"Eva was right before," I began. "This relationship is doomed. You're rich, I'm poor, and if we don't destroy each other now, we will later. We're both too fucked up." I was surprised at my bluntness but not as surprised as Tomaso. He looked at me blankly.

"Was it the sex?"

I shook my head no, but couldn't look at him. Even being near him made me feel queasy. I climbed out of bed on the opposite side from where he sat and headed for the bathroom. The piercing shower spray on my face and chest made me feel better but not good enough. I hoped he'd be gone when I came out. He wasn't. He was looking out the balcony window smoking one of his pretentious Sobranies.

A glossy Italian magazine with his photo on the cover lay half open on the white rug. Did he sit around all day reading about himself, looking at his photos? I wondered for a second what that would feel like. Then, again, I really didn't care. He began talking.

"I used to think affection was just something you felt for pets. That's all I've ever seen around me. Either you are a pet or you own a pet. Either way it's demeaning."

"I really don't want to talk about it."

He turned around. For once he wasn't pulling any tricks with his face but maybe that was a trick too. I thought it strange to see him looking so bland and ordinary, not like Jean-Pierre L'éaud or even like the face on the magazine. Not like anybody.

"But I need to. You owe me that at least." I listened sullenly as I pulled on a pair of jeans I'd found under the bed.

"All my life I've had things handed to me on a silver platter. My parents gave me stuff I didn't even want. When I was a little boy my mom insisted I get a new pair of shoes. The shoes I had on were only a couple months old and I was just starting to like them. I had closets full of shoes. I didn't want any more bloody shoes and I started to make a scene when she dragged me into the shoe store. Then my dad grabbed me and shook me till my teeth rattled. 'Why can't you let us give you anything?' he demanded. 'Why are you so selfish, so ungrateful.' That's how it's been all my life. That's why I dropped out of Cambridge to become an actor. I had to do something on my own for once.

"But do you know the price I had to pay? Can you imagine how many different agents and directors I've had to fuck to get famous? Look at me, Armand!" He grabbed me by the shoulders. "I'm a whore, a cynical, high-priced whore. That's all I am and I never imagined it was possible to be anything else till I met you and Eva."

"So why were you so nasty last night? Don't you have enough guys handing you their asses on a silver platter too?"

Tomaso's eyes shot sparks. He clenched his fists. I was sure, for a second, he'd hit me. Instead, his arms fell to his sides and he just backed away glowering. The silence between us was more painful than a blow. His forehead sweat like olives in the August heat.

"Why does everything have to be so dramatic," I sighed at last. "I said I didn't feel like talking but you had to talk anyway. That's the problem, don't you see? It's always *your* talk, *your* gossip columns, *your* magazine articles, *your* adventures, *your* career."

"Okay," he said, moving his hands nervously over his thighs. "I was wrong last night and I'm wrong now."

"It's not just that."

"What is it then?"

"I don't know. This just feels too heavy. Everything's moving too fast like we're in a speeding car with no brakes."

Tomaso walked back to the window and looked down at the noisy street below. He folded his arms and leaned against the window frame. His silhouette reminded me of a scene from one of his movies, the one where the young revolutionary leans against a window and caresses his arm as he tells his girlfriend that even if one hundred thousand people die in the revolution, their sacrifice will have been worth it. For an instant I wanted to be the girl in that movie, to go over and slip my arms around him. But before I could move, Tomaso turned and, very matter-of-factly asked, "Do you still want me sexually?"

His question threw me. Not only the question but the blasé way he put it, as if asking if I wanted another piece of cake.

"Well?" he pressed, brushing his hair off his face—his best come-and-get-me look.

"Oh, the sex was great," I said, tying my tennis shoe. "First you cocktease me for two months, then you rape me. I can hardly wait to see what comes next."

"Well you can't say I didn't warn you."

Tomaso kicked the magazine with his picture on it into a corner with a pile of others. All tenderness and vulnerability were gone now, discarded like all his other roles.

"I wish somebody had warned me about you though." Did his anger mean he cared?

On the magazine cover Tomaso was smiling, as carefree as the boy next door. He was looking into the camera — at you, me — as if love was oh-so-simple and nothing could tarnish its radiant truth. Thousands of teenage girls had probably pinned it on their bedroom walls by now and were gazing rapturously at it as if it were a healing mandala. But that's not the face Tomaso showed me now. His eyes smouldered with contempt. I tried to answer them.

"I just need some time to be alone."

"Ya, sure."

A dream I'd had a few nights earlier flashed through my mind. I'm standing outside a dark public building feeling utterly lost. I've just stepped from an expensive carriage and am surprised to see I'm wearing all black — top hat, cape, gloves, cane. The cane I especially remember because I was slapping its heavy, carved gold head against my thigh.

The face of my mother, who died when I was seven comes before me. Tears well up in my eyes as I see her bending down to kiss me goodnight. Then the stern, hard face of my father. All my life I've done everything to please him and now I'm even more successful in business than he. I'm so powerful I'm needed at every major government meeting but my heart aches with emptiness. Why? Why am I so wretched when I've done everything he wanted.

This is how I felt walking toward Tomaso's door. He made no effort to stop me. I wished I could say something to erase what I'd said, to start over. I wished he would have grabbed me, hugged me, anything. But he didn't. Tomaso's wall-to-wall carpet felt thick as a snowdrift. My feet felt like lead as I trudged to the door. In the distance I heard a church bell. In my dream I was in Paris.

# Three

When I left Tomaso's I walked the streets in a daze. I felt I'd fallen down an elevator shaft. I crossed the Tuileries, Pont Royal, and stopped to visit Bill in his hotel on the Rue de l'Université. His dry cynicism didn't perk me up. Neither did his small room, which stank of pipe tobacco. He sat on a couch reading, his dirty stocking feet perched on a coffee table. Books, index cards and yellow legal pads — some unused, others full of scribbling — were scattered around him. When I sank into the leather chair across from him, the chair sighed.

"Problems with Eva again?" I'd never told Bill how I felt about Tomaso. He didn't know about Robbie either; a bit late to break the news now. I wasn't sure how sympathetic Bill would be anyway.

"Love is our cross," Bill continued, warming to his favorite topic, "Have some Dubonnet and tell me about it." He poured me a glass from a bottle on the table.

"Nothing much to tell," I replied, taking a sip. "But answer me this. Why would God give us feelings if he didn't want us to use them, or if they can only lead to unbearable pain?"

"Original sin," Bill answered. I might have known. He thought because I'd been to a monastery I shared his views on Faith. I hadn't disabused him of that notion either. Easier to let people think what they pleased. "Some suffering comes from sin and some we can't explain — that's the message of Job — but suffering can purge us of selfishness, excessive rationality, and it can lead us closer to Christ."

I spaced out. Bill's messy room and unshaven face suggested that, for him, suffering was more an excuse than a purification. Bill *liked* suffering. It gave him an identity and made him more like his hero, Erasmus. We smoked some dope, which only made me feel more fragile. I concocted an excuse and, peeling myself away from Bill's sticky leather chair, escaped back to the street.

The afternoon sun blazed. Heat rose up from the pavement making cars and pedestrians appear to be melting, or slowly undulating underwater. I felt separated from this busy, happy world. I felt as if I stood behind a fishtank glass: a world of project and flow on one side; empty stagnation on mine. I phoned Eva but she wasn't home. I kept walking because I didn't know what else to do.

The Luxembourg Gardens looked inviting but I was too restless to sit, so continued down Boul Mich to Daviord's fountain, a fifty-seven foot high monstrosity showing St. Michael fighting a dragon (if only *my* dragon had a face!). A kid in a sleeveless denim jacket offered me some hash, but I shook my head no and meandered on through the honeycomb alleyways of the Rue Git-le-Coeur, where I got a slice of pizza. Then I cut over to the Seine and crossed the Ponts L'Archeveche and St. Louis to Hôtel Lauzen where Daumier, Baudelaire and Rilke once stayed. The pouting stone lion in the courtyard expressed my mood perfectly. From here I crossed the Pont Marie and wandered the Marais till my legs were too tired to go further. It was early evening when I got back to my hotel.

When I got to my room, I tried to write in my journal. What I wrote didn't make sense. I felt as empty as the nobody there in Ionesco's *Bald Soprano* when the doorbell rang. But the love I sought seemed more elusive than any fireman hiding in the bushes.

> *Skip a life and dangle,*
> *turn cartwheels cross the floor.*

*I was feeling kind of seasick*
*when the crowd called out for more . . .*

The lyrics of the new summer hit could be heard from a cafe seven stories below my window. Someone played it over and over every night on the jukebox. Procol Harum's words didn't make sense either, but their music was soothing. So were the cool, rough gray walls of my room. Had Rimbaud agonized in this very spot after quarrels with Verlaine? Yes, Rimbaud knew desperate love, that the self is only liberated outside itself and that, even though we create our objects of desire, they are not nothing. But what are they? What causes anguished love? Bill's answer was worse than none. I decided to write a poem.

> Dear Tomaso, I hate you
> more glorious in your hairy legs
>     than your face.
> Your picture on magazines is a spider
> ensnaring us in its endless web.
> Your angry eyes glisten like treasure.
> Your frightened eyes are two wounds.
> Your seductive eyes promise pleasure
> but all you give is . . .

I couldn't think of a word to rhyme with wound. Tomb or doom sounded dumb, more Poe than Rimbaud. Now I couldn't stop rhyming. I felt as trapped and speechless as I had at Tomaso's. Maybe I'd have to drink absinthe to find a vocabulary or maybe I should give up on words entirely and stick to drawing.

Over the next week the quantity and quality of my artistic work increased. I was especially fascinated with Parisian roofs. Gargoyles, iron latticework framing windows and doors — everything architectural seemed alive. My line was extremely fine, delicate in its suggestion of baroque detail, its rendering of cracks and weather spots. Often I would hide angels by a chimney or window. Although I wasn't the best draftsman, a metaphysical intensity began coming to the fore.

I went to the museum near the Louvre to study Redon, De Chirico and Rousseau. The Louvre itself bored me except for its Puvis de Chavannes and eccentric collection of St. Sebastians. Moving from the twelfth to the fifteenth century, the number of arrows in Sebastian's body increased until he resembled a human pin cushion.

Robbie and Tomaso became my twin demons tunneling from my mind into my nerves, bloodstream and bones. Every person, every building seemed furiously erotic. I wanted to fill my pores with everything.

One afternoon I went to the little park next to L'Eglise de St. Germain to watch children play, I drew cowboys for them, pointed to objects I didn't know the French for, and they would tell me:

 le buisson

 la clôture

 les articles d'épicerie

le moineau

le pistolet

*Un moineau* flew over *le buisson* but I was behind *la clôture*
Nouns I could draw but I couldn't draw verbs. What I
couldn't draw didn't exist. But by drawing I could make
things exist. Everything I drew was *amour.*. Drawing
itself, *amour.* Even my name: Armi, Armand, *amour.*

For a long time I walked until I found myself in a
Métro station. Some anarchists were trying to get com-
muters to rebel against a recent fare increase by throw-
ing smoke bombs. Mistaken for one of their number, *les
flics* chased me into an alley where Marat once lived.
Who was I, the anarchist with me wanted to know.
Jacques was the handsomest of the gang. His unkempt
brown hair framed sharp features, thick sensuous lips
and flashing hazel eyes. He wore torn army fatigues,
suspenders, and a grimy longsleeved thermal undershirt
set off by a red bandanna tied around his neck. His
sweat smelled of danger, excitement.

In my awkward French I tried to explain that I was
a radical too and that I lived nearby in L'Hôtel Monsieur
Le Prince. "*Le concierge là est un cochon,*" Jacques spat.
"A pig!" "*Ah oui,*" I agreed, and I tried to tell of an amusing
encounter I'd recently had at the hotel.

I was late to a class at Alliance Française and,
feeling rushed, had tossed my pan of shaving water out
of the window instead of slowly pouring it as I usually
did. As I bounded downstairs, I bumped into the concierge who was running up.

"*Quel désastre!*" the bald little man gesticulated. "*Il
pleut! Il pleut!*"

My dirty water had landed on his wife's head.
Jacques misunderstood and thought I'd done this on
purpose. Since his group had quarreled with this concierge, he proclaimed me a comrade and invited me to visit
them. He drew a map so I could find their place, which

was in a working class suburb. When he draped his arm over my shoulder I felt wild with desire. I wanted to kiss him, to fall on my knees, to tear open his pants. But there was nowhere we could go and when Jacques saw his friends again, he ran off.

Two days later I made my visit. I left around noon, took the metro to Porte de Vanves, then a bus, then walked the final mile to Jacques' villa. I say "villa" for so I thought he'd described it to me, What I found was a rundown frame house with a yard overgrown with weeds. The front door was locked so I went around to the backyard to read and, when it began to get dark, I climbed in the back window as Jacques told me I could.

I must have fallen asleep for suddenly I was being shaken. Two angry faces stared down at me. Jacques held a candle, another youth a knife. My first thought was of Balzac, my second of the knife which brought a command of French to my tongue which I didn't know I possessed. Once Jacques remembered me we fell into a discussion about the relation of art, sex, and revolution. They believed all three were best when most spontaneous, and that a revolution was soon coming.

It was too late to go back to my hotel so Jacques invited me to stay overnight. They had an extra mattress in the attic. As I followed Jacques upstairs, strange shadows cast by his candle inflamed my desire. "To follow your desire is revolutionary," he'd been saying. I felt we were on the verge of a new era where anything was permissible.

He led me into a room that smelled of pee and set his candle down on a small table. Alone at last, I reached for his crotch. His cock stiffened, he was all cock. But the next thing I knew his fist smashed my face and he spat a word at me that could only mean "faggot." He called for his friend Jean-Paul. My heart pounded. How could I explain my way out of this? When Jean-Paul entered I watched their faces intently. Jacques' lips curled into an evil smile.

He muttered something to Jean-Paul I didn't understand, slowly walked over to me, grabbed me and slammed me into the wall ripping off my shirt. He ordered me to take off my pants. I started to say something, was slapped. *"Ta gueule!"* When I was naked, Jacques grabbed me by the balls and told me to undo his jeans. I realized they intended to use me, maybe worse. My hands shook. When Jacques' jeans were unbuttoned his cock jumped in my face like a beast. He grabbed me roughly by the hair and pushed my mouth down over it. I thought I'd choke. Then he jerked my head back. "Suce-moi la!" he commanded. I worked my tongue for dear life.

Watching all this excited Jean-Paul, who was now himself naked. All of us had lean, hard bodies — Jacques being the most muscular with bicylist's thighs — and despite my fear, my former desire returned. Jean-Paul threw me onto the pee-stained mattress and began ramming his cock down my throat. I sucked like crazy and felt Jacques trying to push his cock up my ass. When it wouldn't go in, he lubricated it with spit and tried again. His cock felt even bigger than Tomaso's. I cried out. This only excited Jacques more and he rammed me so deep I almost fainted. The candle had gone out in the commotion so I could no longer tell who was doing what. The boys' macho inhibitions vanished with the light as did our separate identities. Soon we were squeezing, licking, sucking, slapping, fucking with an energy out of our heads awash in a sea of sweat shit cum grunts squeals of pain and delight.

I must have gone to sleep because I was rudely awakened by Jean-Paul who was on my back fucking me like a locomotive. Automatically I began moving my butt to increase his pleasure. Our moans and vibrations awakened Jacques who started masturbating as he watched. Then he stuck his cock up Jean-Paul's ass. Jean-Paul squirmed, cursed, tried to make him stop but Jacques only fucked harder. I felt I'd be crushed beneath them. When at last Jacques came with a yell and pulled out, Jean-Paul pulled out of me and ran for the bathroom.

Jacques' smooth body was even more breathtaking in the early morning light which filtered in from the dirty attic window. He lay exhausted on his stomach, his arms stretched over his head and dangling over the edge of the mattress. Seeing my chance, I climbed on top of him. Jacques fought like an ocelot, but my lust was greater and when Jean-Paul returned, he ran to help me hold Jacques down. At last I felt my cock ooze into the hot little throne room of Jacques' ass. I told him I was going to fuck him until he moved for me as I had for them. He fought, cursed, cried even but when he saw I meant business he began undulating up and down as erotically as possible to get me to cum, This turned on Jean-Paul so much he started jerking off on us, saving his last load for Jacques' face.

Little trails of sweat and cum ran down our bodies as if we were painted cannibals engaged in some primitive ritual. We were. And we might have gone on like this forever if we hadn't been interrupted by a banging on the front door, Jacques' father yelling he was going to stop paying rent on the place if Jacques didn't return to school. I made a final plunge so deep Jacques shrieked, mixed with my whoop of joy. Then we heard Jacques' father tramping upstairs.

Jean-Paul ran to hold the door as I jumped off the mattress for my clothes. My pants were half on when Jacques' father burst into the room. Imagine his horror — shit and cum smeared everywhere, including his son's face. I dashed past him, down the stairs and into the street, my shoes and torn shirt in my hands. Two blocks later I stopped to put on my shoes. It was a very beautiful morning.

But this little adventure was an exception. Although the orgy certainly whetted my sexual appetite, I was still too shy to cruise strangers. So I threw myself back into drawing. In fact the only time I didn't feel crazy was when I was drawing. I drew St. Anthony running down Boul Mich, his right foot turning into rhubarb. My fingers grazed the sketchpad like the rhizome of a sensitive fern. Only on the page did I feel safe.

When it was too dark to draw, I sat in my room reading or jerking off. Masturbation was pleasurable mainly because, entwining my legs together around my pillow I could imagine myself with Tomaso again. Afterwards, I buried my nose in my sperm-filled hand. How sweet this smell, this taste. It symbolized Tomaso's odor and presence from which, like a Black Magician, I could draw up his very soul.

I still visited Bill occasionally, or had dinner with Eva, but whenever I did, Eva talked about Tomaso, which I hated. I felt she was starting to take Tomaso's side.

"You're so American, so — how do you say — p-purity . . . *Puritan* in your view of love. Why can't you just accept the love he's able to give? Don't you know you're making him suffer?"

"You think *I'm* not suffering?" I slammed down my fork in exasperation. The couple next to us in Le Petit Vatel, the cheap restaurant where we were eating, looked at me with displeasure. Eva was eating brains. I wanted to tell her she was in danger of becoming a cow brain herself; but instead I lowered my voice: "Tomaso knows where to find me. Why should I do all the bending? Besides, you don't know the whole story."

"What is the whole story?" Eva dangled an artichoke leaf in a cup of melted butter. I'd never seen artichokes before Tomaso had bought some for dinner one night. Since I didn't answer, Eva continued. "You walked out on him, remember? He wants to get back together but thinks you don't like him anymore. What happened between you two anyway?"

"He only likes me cause I'm the first guy he's met who he can't manipulate. You were right before. Our backgrounds are too different." But after some further cajoling from Eva, and an admission that yes, I did miss him, I agreed to have dinner with Eva and Tomaso that weekend.

What would it be like seeing Tomaso again? It had been over two weeks since our fight and I was beginning to wonder if I really did want him or was it someone more like Jacques I wanted and were all men except Robbie insufferable shits? Should I just return to the States? In my dreams their faces merged loosening individuality like a bad tooth. Love scuttled across the floor towards me in the shape of a giant cockroach. Maybe I was smoking too much hash. I prayed to our Lady of Perpetual Doubt and went to Eva's dressed as scruffy as possible. She'd moved from her hotel to a sublet on the Place du Commerce. I hadn't shaved in a week.

I smelled a sharp garlic and porcini mushroom sauce as I entered Eva's tiny two-room apartment. Then I saw Tomaso lounging on the couch. He was nursing a glass of red wine and dressed impeccably as usual: white shirt, slacks, sportcoat. We greeted each other awkwardly, each pretending a manic cheerfulness as if nothing had gone awry. Despite freshly cut tulips and a breathtaking view of the square below Eva's balcony, I felt nervous and claustrophobic.

"That Pasolini party really paid off despite everything," Tomaso began gaily. "I've got a good chance for a new Fellini flick and possibly one Fastbender's doing."

"And what'll ya have to pay for that?"

Tomaso looked as if I'd spit on him. For the first time I saw his real face, so hurt I wanted to run over and hug him. But I didn't, couldn't. Why? Why was I so nasty and provocative? Tomaso put on his mask again and Eva shot me a glance from her .45 automatic blue eyes and changed the subject. I became increasingly peevish and irritable.

I walked over to the balcony. Street lights sparkled on the square below, very Henry James only some of the couples strolling together were men. This only made me feel worse. I wanted Tomaso and Eva to feel my pain which was as intense as the red of the tulips. A cool night breeze caressed my face as I poured myself a glass of wine. Tomaso must have brought it, an expensive Côtes de Rhone. Eva and Tomaso were talking in the kitchen and I began to feel they were in league against me because they were jabbering in Italian so fast it sounded like Chinese.[1]

> —*Non ne posso piu. Sono ailo stremo.*
> —*Questo non ha nulla a che vedere con te. Ha dovuto fare qualcosa per salvare la faccia. C'ha detto solo per stozziearci.*
> —*Ha l'aria di essersela Dassata brutta. Sente che c'e un imcomprenensione fra di noi e voglio discuterle a tondo con lui per chiaramento.*
>
> 我讲的话你听得懂听不懂
>
> —*Se riflettiamo insieme dovremmo trovare qualche buona idea.*

Tomaso, who'd come back into the front room during this phrase book dialogue now sat down and began drumming his fingers on the arm of the couch. The tulips seemed to grow redder and redder until it oc-

---

1. Editor's note: this is the translation of what Armand didn't understand:
   —I've really had it. I'm at the end of my rope.
   —This had nothing to do with you. He had to do something to save face. He just said that to get a rise out of you.
   —This misunderstanding between us hurts me and I want to have it out with him. Do you understand what I'm saying?
   —If we put our heads together maybe we can come up with something.

curred to me that maybe Eva and Tomaso were having an affair. They'd probably just asked me over to rub my face in it. 0 stupid me! I didn't know what they were saying but couldn't stand their emptyheaded, exaggerated cheerfulness.

— *Jocca a te Riocane.*

他是你朋友嗎?

— *Dovre smuovere mare e monti per farlo. Quando il carre e sciotto carre come un matto.*[2]

"I know what you bastards are saying," I lied. "Well you'll find this dog has teeth." Eva reddened and Tomaso's jaw went slack. My suspicions were confirmed. I felt sick, paralysed, dead. I had to leave.


Immediately I regretted all my behavior. I wandered the streets wondering if I should go back and apologize. Surely they couldn't destroy my life any faster than I was doing. What about Paris haunted me so?

I returned to Eva's but no one was there. My paranoia increased. It swelled as large as Gargamelle's belly when she was big with Gargantua and, against her husband's advice, consumed sixteen quarters, two bushels, and six pecks of tripe. In this condition I dragged myself to Shakespeare & Company.

Shakespeare's was closed but I saw a note on the door advertising a poetry reading under the Pont Neuf. I went to the bridge and found only a few hippies drinking wine. Ginsberg had been there someone said. I was glad I'd missed him because I was feeling too agitated to listen

---

2. — It's your move. He's your friend.
   — I'll have to move heaven and earth. When the dog is unleashed he runs like mad.

to poetry anyway, I wanted to find Tomaso and beat the shit out of him. I wanted to love him. I wanted to find someone as wild and dangerous as Jacques to kill me.

I went to Montmartre and asked some drag queens how to get to the queer dancing bar. They told me. Their lisping voices made me sick. Soon I'd be outwhoring them all. I hated myself for hating everyone so much but only in frenzied art, sex, or hatred could I survive the pain, I felt even worse than after Robbie's death. Yes, what Tomaso had done to me, and how I missed him now knowing he was still available — this was worse than if he'd died. For death requires no decision. It implies no rejection and demands no forgiveness. Death is irrevocable.

When I got to the bar Eva and Tomaso weren't there but I saw the sullen, beautiful Miriam I'd met in London. She looked like a wasted angel, sadness leaking out of her eyes. She was stoned and didn't remember me. She climbed onto a table. "Any you faggots want this cunt Mick's had a million times?" Someone got her off the table. A cute guy tried to pull me into the can and get me to screw him. I said no 'cause he was such a wimp. Then I said maybe if he bought me some drinks. He started buying me drinks. I gave one to the girl who said she was Miriam Blissful in exchange for a Mandrax. She asked if I wanted to go to a party. I said "Sure." The bartender got us a cab.

Miriam said if she wasn't a junkie she'd be a terrorist. "Would you believe I was an *act*ress once?" Her husky voice slurred like an echo. "I had a *won*derful husband named Peter and a beautiful little boy named *Alexander* and I was per-fect-ly *happy* but Andrew and Peter and everybody wanted me to be a singer. 'I'll make you a *star*' Andrew said, and Mick wrote me a song."

She leaned on my shoulder and started singing softly. "When tears go by . . ." Then she started crying. I wiped her face with a tissue. "Poor Brian," she sobbed. "You're just like Brian. You like me? You like me don't you? You're nice and quiet like Brian used to be . . ."

I rolled down the window. Fresh air blasted my face. Miriam put her hand on my crotch, asked if I'd like to sleep with her. I said maybe but let's wait till we got to the party. I was beginning to wonder if there was a party and what I was doing with this nut who thought she was Miriam Blissful.

"Betcha don't even think I really am who I am," Miriam sobbed, not sobbed actually but laughed only a laugh more heartrending then any tear. A smudge of buildings raced by.

"Well I can prove what I say."

She tore open her silver fox jacket, ripped off her scarf, and showed me a tiny scar on her throat.

"See? That's where they stuck the tubes in me in the hospital."

I knew the story . Her lover had taken her through hell. She'd given up family, friends, singing, and finally her acting career for him and when she was nothing but his mirror he cursed her for her emptiness. He criticized, ridiculed her every move. She tried to leave. He dragged her back. In desperation she reached for a door marked Emergency Exit. For exactly this reason I was afraid of loving Tomaso.

The cab stopped. I paid with money from Miriam's purse as "A Whiter Shade of Pale" poured from an upstairs window. If I'd robbed her blind she wouldn't have known. Following her upstairs I saw her long satin dress looked grimy, yet even in destitution she was heavenly. Her body floated upwards toward the music. The booze and Mandrax were beginning to take effect.

Inside, bodies sprawled over pillows, couches, spilled onto the polished oak floor. The glassy eyes of a polar bear rug stared up at me blankly. Faces I'd seen on record jackets hovered about the room. They could have been painted on balloons.

"Hi everybody!" Miriam announced. "Whatdaya think of my new boyfriend?"

"What's his name?" The icy voice was Tomaso's. His eyes jabbed me like needles. Eva stood frozen at his side.

"Ya, whatchur name honey?" Miriam slurred, hugging my arm like a side rail. I sat her gently on a pillow.

"Tomaso's boyfriend," I said, walking across the room to him. "If he'll have me."

Tomaso looked uncomfortably at Miriam who was trying to rise.

"Howdya find us?"

"Does it matter? Let's go."

I dream I am Mata Hari. Mata Hari isn't my real name but a Balinese stage name I've taken meaning "Eye of Day." I imagine I'm a beautiful dancer but actually I'm just a party hag with a big nose and a big butt. My flirtations are ridiculous. Everyone's smarter than me, which is tragic since I imagine I'm smarter than everyone else.

I try to fool the Germans into thinking I'm a spy to get money but am tricked, framed by Clemenceau's government. The government knows I'm not really a spy but needs to teach the public a lesson traitors won't be tolerated blah blah people laugh at me behind my back until I'm convicted and shot. Then I'm immortalized. I become more beautiful, clever and daring in legend than ever I was alive. When I tell Tomaso this he laughs.

"Wanna hold me off?"

He flexes his arm readying the hypodermic by squirting water across the room. It arcs gracefully hitting the wall with the sound of wet spaghetti. He reminds me of Jamie, the kid in catechism class who once shot the 0 out of Original Sin with his watergun as Sister Madeline chalked it in on the blackboard.

"Sure!"

I squeeze his biceps. His veins, an underground network of rivers, bulge temptingly. This is our ultimate conspiracy, our moment of purest communion,

"Okay," Tomaso says sucking off the needle, "Your

turn."

My veins roll. I'm no longer scared, not like the first few times when I'd done it as a gift for Tomaso. I didn't know then what it meant to be absolutely evil, to think one could build a garden of happiness on other people's backs. I thought I was completely letting go with him, entrusting him with my life in a blood bond as if racing along some cliffside at one hundred miles per hour on a motorcycle. Tomaso was only relaxed when speeding on the edge of death, a contagious transcendent feeling. All the "in" people did it, he said. He was right . . . or so it seemed. How long had I been living with him now — five months, six? We'd been in Berlin, Rome . . . Tomaso pinned down my elusive vein and entered it.

I watched my blood spurt suddenly into the needle. My translucent being oxidized into a beautiful wine dark sea. *Hoc est enim corpus meum . . . Hic est enim calix sanguinis mei.* The words of Consecration flooded back to me from childhood. "Do this as oft as you shall drink it, in Memory of Me." Then for the booster, in and out, my blood buzzing higher and higher until Tomaso slowly lifts his hand off the top of my head and I'm totally beyond, dangling euphorically in outer space as never before except right after the first time I made love to Robbie. Walls melted.

"Howdya feel?"

Tomaso grins his little boy smile, the one that first captivated me. His face appears as a succession of angels: Pharzuph (angel of lust), Pesagniyah (who, when prayers of persons in deep sorrow ascend, kisses and accompanies them to a higher region), Affafniel (Prince of sixteen faces, four on each side of his head, that constantly change their aspect). I cannot speak, just smile. My strobing eyes settle into his. Tomaso slowly reaches out his hand and our fingers clasp. Our eyes focus on a region no one else can see.

# Four

Some of the names for heroin are brown sugar, candy, chasing the dragon, horse, H, henry, junk, liquid sky, mama, milk of paradise, scag, shit, smack and snow, though this last usually signifies cocaine for the sound of sleighbells one hears after shooting it. What it's called matters little for whatever name it parades under, it leads to the same narrow basement of oblivion where every human value is numbed, perverted, twisted — obliteration of all need except the need to end need. Entropy! Then one waltzes underwater as in the river Lethe. Few who enter this kingdom ever escape, for from blood-red poppy to white lime of mummification, heroin is the coward's road to suicide.

"Can the Snow Queen come in here?" asked the little girl.

"Just let her come," said the boy, "and I will put her on the stove where she will melt."

There was a real world out there. A revolution was going on. It came and went, but the world of time was not ours. Tomaso and I were like shades in a dream. We felt no pain, but could only get it on when stoned; then it was intense, utterly unreal. I'm not sure we knew or cared who was fucking us at parties sometimes. Often we just held hands and kissed while strangers plowed us from behind.

I remember one party presided over by the filmaker Fastbender. Although only twenty-seven, four years older than I, he was already dictatorial and obnoxious. His breath stank almost as bad as his unbathed body, which exuded that sour odor peculiar to drug addicts. Tomaso wanted desperately to work with him. Despite Fastbender's foul stench, Tomaso sat as close to him as possible. Fastbender took this courtship as his right and, inbetween chain-smoking Camels and guzzling Heinekens, blathered about upcoming film projects.

"*Siddhartha*! I've always wanted to do that. What tale better exemplifies the bourgeois German dream? A sensitive youth leaves a protected religious environment to find himself in the world." Fastbender turned his puffy, unshaven face toward me and winked. My monastic background was well known and a frequent source of amusement.

"So our kid goes through a city whose walls are smeared with shit, real shit, not this street graffiti which is springing up everywhere, but wanting more he walks on. He comes to a forest of monumental erections, then a desert where intimacy has been abolished.

"On the desert's edge he encounters a tree, a brook, a bird, and a woman of pleasure. All are eager to school him. The tree grows, the brook bubbles, the bird sings and flies. Ah, the wonders of nature! But best of all is the woman who signs him up for special classes: Nipple biting 112, Cocksucking 205 . . ."

"Her educational methods aren't European but American let's hope," Tomaso interjected. "I mean, is education for the student or vice versa?"

Tomaso's wit was at my expense but I couldn't complain since I was now living off him. Fastbender roared with laughter. "Ach! Uppers to sleep on, betrayal to survive. That's the way with us queers isn't it. Europe spawned Dadaism but how could it compete with America's Doggie Diner heads and MacDonald's Golden Arches? Dadaism simply couldn't survive as an oppositional movement in a society whose entire being strained to imitate Duchamp's toilet."

Here the director paused to eat some snot from his nose. The gesture signaled not only his supreme confidence but also his supreme contempt. I thought of the yogi who, after scolding his colleagues, was asked if *he* was free of defilement. "He who tries to get out only sinks deeper," replied the yogi. "I roll in it like a pig. I digest it and transform it into golden dust or a brook of pure water. To fashion stars out of dog dung, that's the Great Work!"

"So what of the tree, brook, bird and woman of pleasure?" Fastbender continued. "Shall we plant them in America? Shall we bequeath them to Wim Wenders to symbolize a floating crap game of the decline and fall? Or shall we make these figures garish images of purity in a corrupt, decaying regime? Oh poor things! In any event their act doesn't get the kid off so everyone prays to Jesus to find out what's wrong. No sooner does Jesus show his face with just a trace of pubescent beard than Siddhartha sprouts an erection right through his pants, the veins of it pulsing like strobe-lights in a suburban rock festival."

"I'd love to play Jesus sometime," Tomaso again interrupted.

"You would eh?" Fastbender's eyes narrowed making the smile under his mustache more ominous. "Jesus?" He giggled. Then he let loose a Teutonic roar.

"BUT HOW CAN YOU IF *I* AM HE? NO MATTER HOW MUCH I INVITE YOU TO SHARE IN THE PAIN OF MY CRUCIFIED SOUL, STILL YOU MUST LOVE ME, *ADORE* ME . . . ADMIT IT, DON'T YOU ALL ADORE ME?"

Everyone's head bobbed as the director stood. His beer gut sagged over his worn leather belt, as he blasted us with his rotting vegetable breath. He was still punching his stubby forefinger at us but was now yelling fiercely at Tomaso.

"YOU ARE FAMOUS. EUROPE REVERES YOUR NAME. HOLLYWOOD WAITS, STILL THE CONFIDENT SEDUCTRESS. BUT INSTEAD OF MAKING FILMS THERE, YOU ARE HERE, TRAPPED IN THIS VORA-CIOUS LIFE. AND LIKE ALL AWARE PEOPLE OF OUR

TIME, YOU TAKE DRUGS SEEING THAT ART CAN NO LONGER BE JUSTIFIED AS A SUPERIOR ACTIVITY, OR EVEN AS AN ACTIVITY OF COMPENSATION TO WHICH ONE CAN HONORABLY DEVOTE ONESELF. THE CAUSE OF THE DETERIORATION IS CLEARLY THE EMER-GENCE OF PRODUCTIVE FORCES THAT NECESSI-TATE OTHER PRODUCTION RELATIONS AND A NEW PRACTICE OF LIFE . . ."

Here the director paused to wipe a dirty handker-chief over his sweaty face. He delivered his last words in a hoarse whisper which seemed only to intensify their force.

"So for the love of God, show us some *real* acting. Make your little Siddhartha here come to life."

Tomaso began to undo my pants. For some time now I had taken to wearing his jeans and leather jacket. I luxuriated in the connotations of their smell: brute, biker, barbarian, cop. But more, I felt it was my only way to get inside Tomaso, to get literally inside his skin. So too, in Albania, sick infants were sewn inside the bellies of newly slaughtered cows, then cut out as if receiving a second birth.

When my, or rather Tomaso's jeans fell to my ankles, I felt myself rise to the ceiling so as to better view this tableau in which I was the central prop. Tomaso got on his knees and began sucking me off. I felt nothing. Nothing happened. The crowd registered its disappoint-ment.

"Stick a finger up his ass, maybe that'll help," someone snickered. A well known French actor ambled into the kitchen with Gunther Hoffman, "my Bavarian Negro," as Fastbender called him.

"I more or less agree with the Situationists," the Frenchman said. "They say it's all finally integrated. It gets integrated in spectacle. It's *all* spectacle!"

"Then our role as artists is to steal the show," Hoffman replied.

Fastbender's friends delighted in the spectacle of

our humiliation because usually it was they who bore the brunt of his "jokes." One hand slapped me hard on the butt as another tore open my shirt and twisted my nipple. Then a new prop entered the fray.

"Here, try this."

A bright silver tube about fifteen inches long and a little less than a half inch wide was placed in Tomaso's hands. On one end was a flashlight switch.

Tomaso looked at me with a "Gee-I-really-hate-to-do-this" grimace and turned me around. Lubricating the device he inserted it gently up my anus. My ass tingled pleasurably at first and I thought I might enjoy cumming. Then a searing fire tore up my spine. I jumped two feet forward and passed out.

In having a bad protector, as I imagined I'd been for Robbie, I sought to become more like Robbie. This dynamic had happened before — maybe Tomaso sensed I wanted it — and it related to why I'd entered the monastery in the first place. I wanted to empty myself of everything, to give myself wholly to the Other. Like Robbie, I wanted to be a saint, but a saint in a world without God.

Regardless of how Tomaso treated me I still loved him, even more now for his cowardice. If he'd ignored or abandoned me, that would have been unbearable; but in ridiculing and abusing me, he showed he still cared. I'd cast my lot.

Parties blurred as did the cities we lived in — Rome, Munich, Barcelona. Each new city, each new movie Tomaso made, each new set of friends were going to be a new beginning but each new scene turned out to be like the old ones. Then Tomaso began hanging out with a well known rock singer and his wife whom, for reasons that will soon be obvious, I shall refer to only as K. and A. Tomaso needed a rest after a Visconti film he'd just finished so, along with Miriam Blissful, we accepted an invitation to stay at the mansion K. had just leased at Villefranche, a fishing village on the southern coast of

France. A vacation, Tomaso said. Someplace where we could just sail and relax.

Our new friends had just moved from England, mainly for tax reasons but also because of a disturbing incident they'd had with Kenneth Anger. Anger was into Black Magic as well as filmmaking. A., who was rumored to be into Black Magic herself, wore a garlic necklace to protect herself from him.

Before leaving, Tomaso, Miriam and I stopped at one of the summer homes of Tomaso's father, a stiff, formal man who seemed proud of his son's success while at the same time disapproving of it. While his manner was gracious, he betrayed what he thought of me by occasionally raising his eyebrows as if discovering a stain on his dining room lace. But you don't truly know someone until you see how they are with their mother.

Mrs. Bianchi, I could tell, had once been a great beauty. Watching her glide into a room or put everyone at ease simply by raising a glass to her lips made me realize he mostly took after her. But when the three of us were alone together she changed. "Tommy," she'd coo. "Aren't you going to give mamma a kiss?" And he would. Or "Tommy, why do you *insist* on wearing those *horrid* old sneakers without socks? You're doing it just to spite me, aren't you?" Then she'd sigh. "Maybe he'll listen to you, Armand. I can't get him to do anything anymore." Although she spoke with an air of resignation, I knew — and she made sure I knew she knew — that I'd never have the influence over her son that she did. Tomaso might wince, but he always did what she wanted. Indeed, he played the dutiful son so brilliantly that Mr. Bianchi insisted on sailing us to Villefranche in his yacht.

Lush gardens of grapes, nectarines, bananas, palm, and rubber trees spilled down to K. and A.'s private jetty. We disembarked, waved goodbye to Tomaso's father, and climbed the flagstone steps like kids adventuring to an ogre's castle. When we reached the patio, which encircled the Spanish Mediterranean villa, we even held hands and skipped. Maybe things *would* improve in this idyllic setting.

Miriam pounded on the carved doors. When no one answered, we went in. Large oak and marble panelled rooms were stuffed with thick Persian carpets, Ming vases and other antiques; a decor no more opulent than Tomaso's family's but decidedly more ostentatious. In one room everything was covered in Naugahyde except a couch covered in white mink. The whole house seemed to say "Look, my owners are wealthy," yet despite this opulence and a steady stream of visitors, I soon discovered that K. and A. mostly stayed in their bedroom shooting junk.

The evening we arrived, K. and A. presided over an early dinner of turtle soup, salmon mousse and quail. Miriam and Giselle Glèves sat next to Tomaso and Eric and an ex-racing driver named Tommy and his wife.

Watch how K. watches A.," Michele whispered. "I think he suspects she had a fling with Mick but he's afraid to confront her. That's why he looks like he's about to explode." She giggled.

"Wine making you tipsy?" K. challenged. "Must be if you think you can make it with that flaming rentboy." Tommy guffawed, which reddened his big ears and coarse Irish face. Later I learned he'd smuggled a kilo of coke into the country under his kid's clothes.

"What K. means is that Armi's an American who spent several years in a monastery," Tomaso interjected trying to lighten the atmosphere. At the word monastery, A.'s face lit up.

"An artist too, I hear," K. sneered. "Well, let's get some target practice in while there's still some light."

When not involved in games of infidelity or violence, K. spent at least an hour every day shooting vases off the patio balustrade with a .45. K. and A. enjoyed initiating minors into the world of drugs and kinky sex. A. in particular believed one gained in Magic power only to the extent one was willing to break taboos. When the daughter of their French chef became violently ill after A. shot her up, A. decided it might be better to scout further afield for subjects. Tomaso and I were recruited to help.

It was late afternoon when A. and I neared Nice in a carmine red Jaguar E-type convertible. Tomaso followed in K.'s KJ6. Two farmboys about fourteen and sixteen stood by the road, their thumbs extended like newly bloomed sexual organs. It didn't take much to get them to agree to join us for a "party" or, upon returning to the villa, to sniff a little smack. Soon afterwards they passed out.

"Aren't they little gluttons," A. yawned. "And so dirty too. Look at the smudges they made on my nice white couch. Well we can't leave them here can we? Bring them to the cellar and let's clean them up."

"Can't we fix first?" Tomaso pleaded. "Snorting this shit doesn't do anything for me." A. stood up, her straight blond hair falling past her shoulders and framing her strong, Nordic features. If she wore a helmet, she'd look like a Viking.

"Me neither, hon. But first we work, then play. House rules."

Tomaso knew better than to argue. He lifted the older boy up by his armpits, I grabbed the boy's legs, and we stumbled along behind A. down to the wine cellar. After getting both boys downstairs, we stripped them of their clothes and fastened their wrists and ankles into leather straps that had been attached to wooden pillars that buttressed the ceiling.

"What are you planning?" I asked uncertainly.

"Oh, just some fun," A. replied casually, sponging off the boys' dusty bodies. "Umm," she murmured as their tan lies grew sharper. "These little butts look like double scoops of vanilla ice-cream."

"Just the dainty dish to set before the Queen," Tomaso quipped. I glared at him.

"Okay, that's fine for now," A. said. "You guys can

run and do your thing. We'll play our games tomorrow."

When Tomaso and I got back to our room, I shut the door and unloaded my concerns. Some vacation! First Tomaso's parents and now this. I didn't know who was creepier: K. with his macho bullshit or A. with her sleazy deviousness. They both made me sick.

"You make me sick with your constant complaining too," Tomaso retorted. "If those punks weren't here, where'd they be? Off banging pussy or bashing fags. And why are you here? Because you really love me or because I've got money and can cart you all over Europe to meet and draw famous people?"

"Shit! If you don't believe I love you . . ."

"Sure I believe it. But I don't *know* it. I can't know anything, especially when all you do is bitch all the time. And talk about sleaze! You weren't so pure with those anarchists either. So relax. Let's just fix and then we can make love or walk down to the beach or do whatever you fucking want."

With that, Tomaso shot up. Then he shot me up. Whatever had bothered me before didn't matter anymore. To be high and in Tomaso's arms was heaven.

The next morning K. flew to Switzerland to get his blood changed. It was the only way he could abide cleaning up for a concert tour. This left A. the next couple of weeks to do whatever she wanted. Maybe it was because I was loaded, but her games didn't seem as bad as I'd first feared. One was called "Guess Which Hole." A boy would stick his cock through a hole in a blanket behind which was Tomaso's mouth, A.'s cunt or my ass. If the boy guessed the orifice correctly, he'd get to fuck A. If not, Tomaso or I would get to fuck him.

Another game was called "Cover All Bases." The boys would be given acid and shown stag films till they were peaking and horny as hell. Then one boy would be invited to eat out A.'s pussy while I sucked him off and

108

Tomaso fucked him. Every few minutes we'd change positions till all the bases had been covered.

But this wasn't enough for A. One night we unwound from a coke binge by gulping a few Mandrax followed by swigs of Courvoisier. Within an hour we'd passed out, heaped on top of each other on K. and A.'s oversized Louis XIV bed. I awakened to the sound of bouncing springs. A. was balling Tommy, the race driver, as his wife lay zonked out beside him. When I later told Giselle about this, she warned me not to let K. find out.

"He's scared shitless of his wife," she said. "He'll only take his rage out on you."

Giselle told me of an earlier houseguest who'd died mysteriously after running afoul of A. Was the power of Black Magic real? Did A. put hexes on her enemies? Giselle and Miriam thought so. This especially bothered me because A. told Tomaso she expected us to help her with a Black Mass that weekend. "Thank god Miriam and I will be gone by then," Giselle said when I told her. "Group sex is too powerful for me, even without the Magic."

Group sex, I discovered, was itself an addiction, a thrill not unlike shooting drugs. When lying naked in pitch darkness with three to six others, particularly if of mixed gender, it becomes strangely impossible to tell whose body is whose. Sometimes I couldn't even identify my own arms or legs or where the boundaries of my body were unless I pinched myself. Even then I couldn't always tell.

So who *am* I in such a situation?

One becomes group body, group mind. One melts into the whole group's lust, delirium, hunger, energy and exploration. As perceptions of bodily boundaries dissolve, so does the conscious "I." This feels tremendously liberating. Concepts such as male/female, black/white, gay/straight, arm/leg lose meaning as if devoured by a higher power. Smells, tastes, sounds, feelings, bodily fluids — everything rearranges and intensifies in a wild, playful frenzy. I'd grown so accustomed to orgies that making love to anyone alone, even Tomaso, seemed bland by comparison.

"It isn't group sex I'm against," I said to Tomaso the next morning. "It isn't even the games we've been playing with those boys. What bothers me is A.'s demonic power over us. I feel she's draining our souls."

"*Souls*?" Tomaso laughed, splashing his feet in the water under the jetty where we sat. Waves slapped the red fiberglass speedboat which was tied to the jetty and I could hear K. and A.'s macaws squawking in their cages behind the palm and banana trees. The morning sun was hot and as dazzling as a ciborium. I felt silly to be fussing in such a paradise.

"The little monk in you is peeping out again, Armi. Rather we go to a church camp?"

"I'm serious," I persisted. "I you *don't* think A. has evil power over us, let's prove it by leaving tonight with Giselle and Miriam."

"What? And mess up not only my best set of career connections but all this free coke and scag? Shit! You don't have enough to buy one snort of anything. Look at yourself, Armi. You're a junkie! Leave now and you'll be crawling back by morning just begging for a fix."

All the excuses I'd protected myself with fell like a house of cards: that I mainly "just snorted," or that on bad mornings I "just had a little flu." My escape from society had become the worst prison of all. I wasn't just empty. I was damned. Tomaso's voice softened as he lifted up my chin with his thumb and forefinger.

"I don't mean to be nasty, Armi, but you knew the life I led before you teamed up with me. And I *do* love you. If it wasn't for you . . ."

At this he pulled me close, hugging me gently and nuzzling my ear with his tongue. Even now I adored him — his baby smooth skin, his strong firm muscles. In his arms I still felt safe, although if I'd thought I could give ballast to his life I'd failed. But he didn't complain. He

110

simply whispered "I love you" over and over. Those words I'd yearned so long to hear I now detested. Love too was a prison. And I hated myself most of all.

By Saturday the only ones left were A., two servants, Tomaso and I, and the boys. The servants were closing down the house since A. was flying to join K. in Switzerland on Monday. What vampires they were: K., paying $5,000 to change all the blood in his body so he could tour the States and make millions more for debauchery, and A., living off him, us, anyone she could sink her hands into.

All day A. stayed in her room. What she did I don't know. Maybe she watched soaps or maybe she worked spells and invocations. My earlier conversation with Giselle had set me to thinking of the old ornate chest in A.'s room. She guarded it so jealously I assumed it was her drug stash. Once, when she and K. were gone, I saw she'd forgotten the key. It lay on the bed, studded with rubies. Usually she wore it around her neck on a black velvet ribbon. I'd assumed at first it was just an odd piece of antique jewelry.

I glanced up and down the hall. No one was around. I crept in the room, picked up the key and opened the chest. A noxious, rancid odor overwhelmed me. Indeed, the entire room smelled like a garbage pit heaped as it was with dirty clothes and plates of mouldy food. But the odor from the chest was more powerful. Bits of bone with fur and flesh rotting off mixed with a sickeningly sweet smell that exuded from a box of black candles. I smelled narcissus, patchouli, formaldehyde. Pungent odors I'd never encountered before seeped out from under the caps of strange bottles: dark oils, grey-green unguents, pink and yellow powders. One large bottle looked as if it was filled with blood. I slammed down the lid and returned A.'s key to the bed. I'd forgotten this until now.

At about 3 p.m., Tomaso and I were summoned into A.'s bedchamber. Her disembodied voice wafted toward us from behind a tall black and red lacquered Chinese screen.

"The ceremony will begin at midnight," she said. "Your instructions are in an envelope by the door. Anything else you need I'll give you later. Prepare the boys too. I suggest you take a nap now so you'll be rested."

At A.'s mention of the boys my stomach tightened. Their early rebelliousness had been swiftly and harshly punished. They'd since been given enough drugs to keep them pliable. As their imprisonment continued, they began to participate in A.'s games with such enthusiasm that I was reminded of circus dogs leaping through hoops. "All men should be taught so well," A. laughed after one playful session. I thought of K., barking and sniping at guests during our first dinner together but cringing and looking down every time A. looked at him.

The servants left the house after dinner. At 11:30 p.m., Tomaso and I appeared at A's door, naked under our black cassocks and lace surplices as she'd instructed. We entered the room to find A. standing naked. Considering how she abused her health, she was still stunningly beautiful. Her body was tanned, her muscles well toned. Her long blond hair shimmered in the candlelight which doubled its reflection off two wall sized mirrors facing each other. I saw three of her, three of us. It wasn't easy to tell which figures were real.

A set of black leather vestments was spread out on the bed. We helped her into them. As we did so, she sprinkled droplets from a silver aspergillum over everything mumbling incomprehensible phrases in a rhythmic cadence. She seemed to be in a trance as urine splashed from the shaker. When we finished dressing her, Tomaso and I each picked up a brass candle holder in which burned a three foot tall black candle. Then we led the way downstairs while A. dipped her shaker into a silver bowl and sprinkled it eclesiastically to her right and left.

The ceremony itself followed the usual pattern of inverting Roman Catholic ritual over the body of a whore. Instead of whores, the boys were strapped stomach down on the makeshift wine cellar altar. During the Confiteor, Tomaso and I fucked them as A. sprinkled us all with her silver shaker. Then she confessed to Satan for any act of soft-heartedness she'd ever displayed.

When we got to the Consecration, A. held up a goblet of the boys' sperm she'd been collecting. She spit into it and added a dash of wine. It must have been a considerable amount judging by how deeply she drank.

"SATANUS VOBISCUM!'" she cried, wine and sperm drooling down her chin.

"Eat cum spittle too some more," Tomaso and I mumbled in response.

Then, to my astonishment, A. pulled a live chicken from a crate hidden under the altar. She had so much trouble holding the frightened bird down while Tomaso chopped its head off that I almost broke into giggles. The bird clawed wildly till A.'s arms ran red with blood. Then, trying to hold the headless, spastic chicken steady by the wings, she commanded Tomaso to lift up her leather chasuble while she inserted its thrashing neck into her vagina. It wasn't easy and she had trouble standing still — a scene so horrid it was funny. I probably would have laughed out loud but when A. finished, she used the bird on the boys. Now I felt like vomiting. I'm sure I would have if it hadn't been for what happened next.

Having lubricated the boys with chicken blood mixed with our sperm, the demented harridan tossed the flapping bird aside and began to shove her greased hand into the anus of the boy nearest her. Even though his mouth was taped and Tomaso'd shot him up with MDA just an hour before, I could tell by how his eyes bulged that he was in agony. It was more than I could bear. While Tomaso stood frozen in shock I screamed "Stop it you witch! This is going too far!"

"Too far?"

A. looked around the wine cellar like she didn't know where she was and I felt a palpable wind fill the room and push against my chest. Then I heard an unnaturally deep voice spill from A.'s lips.

"NO, NO . . . NEVER TOO FAR!"

A gleam lit up her eyes that I'd seen only once before, a look so terrible I shall never forget it — Theodosius! My blood turned to ice. I cried out the one word that linked these two experiences.

"ROBBIE!"

The entire room seemed to heave a sigh of relief as I heard a great flapping of wings like a flock of seagulls taking off. A.'s arms fell listlessly to her side. Then a smell of honeysuckle hit my nostrils, the smell of a summer evening's pollen-laden air, and finally, rising over and above it, a sharp, sweet smell of boyish sweat that was unmistakable. From somewhere, from the slaughtered chicken perhaps, a long white feather fell at my feet. But I knew better. Robbie had answered my cry.

"Take A. upstairs," I commanded Tomaso. "Then let's free these kids and split."

For once Tomaso followed my orders instead of I his. He took A. by the arm and led her upstairs as if she were a zombie. I cut the kids loose, then phoned the police. When Tomaso came back downstairs he panicked.

"The cops? We're foreign junkie accomplices to kidnapping and you call the cops? Christ!"

I held up a key. "But we won't be here when they come. The speedboat's docked at the jetty, right? I packed our stuff earlier. So let's get our bags and split."

I wasn't as stupid as Tomaso thought. I knew it would take drastic action to get him to leave. By the time A. would be coherent enough to put the cops on our tail, we'd hopefully be out of the country. I had no money myself, of course, but Tomaso did and I also knew he'd be unstinting when it came to saving his own skin.

I'll spare you the details of how we got to Rome. Our drug withdrawal was more difficult. We tried to cut back, Tomaso resumed working and I started drawing again. Although we were often irritable, we never mentioned

Villefranche. There were rumors, but Tomaso's agent concocted a story that we'd been in the Bahamas. (People will say anything if you pay them enough.) K. and A. had too much trouble of their own to go after us. Rome had its own dangers.

The strain of work and our relationship gradually pulled us back to our excesses. Tomaso could do anything, even commit atrocities, but only on heroin could he call himself my lover. How unbearably painful too our last night together, those last images which begat one another like the endless list of Moses' forefathers.

Images.

Images falling from the sky like shards of the demon's mirror. And like parting shots of a slow motion film sequence, the final frames played through my dreams for weeks:

Staggering . . . neck and face a flaming bruise . . . rasping through clenched teeth "I think it was c-cut with — " . . . collapsing into a ratty couch, his head rolling back, his eyes bulging, his body convulsed . . . drag queens passed out on quaaludes, their '40s furs serving as doormats . . . someone bursting in "Where is he? We gotta call an ambulance quick." Another voice "No, just get him outta here" . . . my own voice eerily distant from me as I touched his face . . . .

I could take no more. As I waited in the hospital (long corridors. a medicinal smell, pale yellow walls, high ceilings) I decided that whatever happened I had to leave. So when the doctor came out and said Tomaso was out of danger, I went back to our hotel and phoned Eva.

"Armi!"

Her voice registered surprise, concern. (Armies of what?) Or was it her pause afterwards that suggested this? I couldn't blame her. We hadn't written or phoned, not even when she and Bill sent a wedding announcement. I hoped we'd at least sent a present but what, a fondue set?

"I know I've been a shit," I began. "My life's such a

mess I don't know what to do. I feel like killing myself. If you slam the phone down on my ear I can't say I'd blame you."

Manipulative, yes, but I was too desperate to care. In the back of my mind — ha! Such chaos churned there I felt weirdly detached, yet connected, like a surfer riding waves of some unspeakable . . . .

"Where are you, Armand? What's wrong?"

Eva sounded more awake now. How much could I tell her? Should I talk about the siren, the men in white coats who gently but hurriedly had lifted Tomaso onto a stretcher and into the ambulance, the cold plastic seats of the taxi? I could hardly keep my pain back now — rain, night breaking into daylight, streetlights glowing leprously, the hiss of tires on wet pavement. Suddenly I remembered skipping home in the rain when I was seven. I hated the feel of my feet in those squishy, wet shoes but since I couldn't do anything about it, why not throw up my arms and jump around. While I mumbled incoherently to Eva I massaged my arm, neck and shoulder squeezing the muscles deeply as if trying to convince myself this wasn't just another dream.

"What's your phone number," Eva pressed. "You have money don't you? Okay, I want you to call the airport and book the first available flight to Paris. Will you do that, Armand?"

The way she said this reminded me of my grand-mother who covered everything in the house: walls, floors, windows, every table and chair. I shut my eyes and envisioned Early American scenes in sepia on the wallpaper, thick '40s drapes with rose colored flowers and dark green leaves. These associative blips I remember better than what Eva and I were saying.

When I got off the phone to Eva I called the airport. Then I wrote Tomaso a note: "Dear Tomaso, It's not your fault but . . . ."

I didn't know what else to say. Maybe that was enough. In the suitcase my clothes and notebooks looked like a pyramid of past lives — until I closed the lid, that is, and sat on it so I could fasten the snaps. Too bad I couldn't stuff my feelings as easily. Then I made another stab at the note.

"Dear Tomaso, You probably won't believe this but I still . . ." Still what — loved him, believed love was possible? Still waters done reap, as the saying goes, or something like that.

# Between Worlds

# One

How different this flight into Paris. Even on Valium I had the shakes. If Bill and Eva hadn't been at the airport to meet me, I doubt I could have made it through customs.

I expected Bill to be distant, if not accusatory, but marriage seemed to have mellowed him. He didn't hug me as Eva did but he smiled broadly, shook my hand, and grabbed my bag. Solid, that's the word. Bill seemed more serene and solid. His shoulders filled out his tan sportcoat more and he walked briskly.

Eva glowed. She seemed more centered and relaxed, too. Soon I found out why. She showed me a photo of their child, Andrea, who was almost two and had big blue eyes and blond hair like her mom. For a moment I envied them but heterosexuals can be screwed up too (I'd certainly met plenty in Tomaso's circle, not to mention in America — my parents, for instance). Mostly I felt relief. I'd been so dumb to take Eva and Bill for granted.

Then we were outside — trees turning red and yellow in the crisp air. It's hard to be depressed in Paris in early autumn. Bill and Eva walked me to their Renault and we drove to their new place on the Rue Poulletier. Bill had gotten the place through a friend. His book on the Free Spirits had been a success — popularly as well as academically — and he'd gotten a grant, which had enabled him and Eva to stay on in Paris.

"So how do you like it?" Eva asked when we were inside.

Late afternoon sunlight poured in through two large bay windows facing the street. A crystal hanging from the top of one refracted a mandala of color onto a tan corduroy couch. A large gray vase of calla lilies, ginger, and birds-of-paradise sat on a black art decco coffee table in front of the couch. Lots of plants too — ferns, African violets, diffenbachia, wandering Jews, and a six foot tall rubber plant.

"I don't know what to say," I replied at last. "Your place is so warm and beautiful. *You're* so warm and beautiful."

"It's warmer still having you back with us," Eva said, pinching me. "Say, remember this?"

Eva put on a Billie Holliday album, one I'd bought her the summer we first met (". . . I know somewhere Spring must fill the air with sweetness just as rare as the flower that you gave me to wear" and "Hush now, don't explain . . ."). Then she took me to the guest room, which she'd fixed up for me. It was neat and cozy with a small bookcase, a single bed and a window overlooking a back garden. Over the bed, in a stainless steel frame, hung the charcoal drawing of Chartres I'd given Eva three and a half years ago.

"Gosh I . . . I mean ."

"Don't worry," Eva said. "Just rest. There'll be plenty of time for us to talk later."

Eva was right. Talk was the last thing I wanted to do right then though what I wanted — besides stopping taking drugs and starting my life over — I wasn't sure. If I made a quick list it might have looked like this:

| | | |
|---|---|---|
| to bathe | to let go of pain | to rage |
| to breathe | to forget | to isolate |
| to rest | to dissolve | to run away |
| to pray | to cry | to fight |
| to unpack | to curse | to fuck |
| to wait | to scream | to sneak some drugs |
| to walk | to hide | to stop thinking |
| to write | to bitch | to go to sleep |
| to weep | to find even one | to sleep forever |
| | brief moment of serenity | |

I settled on sleep. Lying down with my clothes on, I pulled a comforter over me and buried my head deep under a pillow.

O sweet floating cavern of imagined night, lulled by darkness (dark lullaby, song of my imagined mother — Eva), let your dream caravans meander over me (my soul, a parched and febrile desert) like the casual piano back-up on those old Billie Holliday records. Yes, that old bluesy, heroin-blurred voice digging into a pain so deep it finally hit a nerve of something so absolutely pure and primal that it gushed up into the transformative oasis of song.

And suddenly I recalled (or some glimmer in me did, another random neuron flash) an early rare Caruso record of Tomaso's wherein the pianist got so enraptured, so totally carried away by Caruso's voice that he forgot to stop playing. Caruso stopped singing, the song was finished, but the piano tinkles on for several more ghostly measures. That's how my love for Tomaso had gone. Then, mercifully, sleep swept over me like a wave.


"Get up, Armi. Get up."

I felt a tugging at my sheet and woke to see little Andrea trying to crawl up onto my bed.

"Get up," Andrea tugged at me again. "I wan eat."

Lifting my eyelids as if they were heavy garage doors, I squinted at her. Her eyes were wide and bright as morning. I felt her sparrow heartbeat on top of me now, her blue corduroy coveralls wet.

"You need to go tee-tee potty?"

"Tee-tee potty, gooey potty," Andrea chirped, sliding off my bed and toddling for the bathroom. "Light on," I heard her say as she flipped the switch. Was there a heaven for all the gooey potty children everywhere so lovingly bestow on their parents? Perhaps this was the beginning of culture. Soon it would be "See my drawing," and later "Would you like to read my novel?" Perhaps children's joy — if one could open up to it — offered a better cure for drug or love addictions than could any psychiatrist or priest.

Over the next couple of weeks Andrea's bubbly enthusiasm, Eva's wholesome cooking and quiet nurturing, and Bill's new upbeat personality began to pull me out of my gloom. First I was one day clean, then two days, and finally two weeks. Tomaso was probably my main addiction. That's why I couldn't stand watching him kill himself. I had to show him it was possible to stop and the only way I could do that was to separate for a while. And the only way I could do *that* was to focus all my attention and energy to staying off drugs. It wasn't easy but within two weeks I was amazed at how much better I felt — physically as well as emotionally.

"This is what I used to take drugs to feel like," I told Eva one morning.

"Well keep it up," she replied. "You look a lot better too. But don't get cocky. Just keep exercising and take it one day at a time."

My daily schedule was now as follows: at eight-thirty I'd walk Andrea five blocks to her daycare center. At ten I'd walk across town to Bill's gym to go swimming. The first half lap I'd swim underwater for purification. After about fifteen laps I'd read or draw until one when I'd pick up Andrea who I'd watch till three or four when either Bill or Eva'd had returned home. Then I'd jog to the Luxembourg Gardens and back or take the Métro to Pére Lachaise and jog in the cemetery. (Apollinaire, Daumier, Isadora Duncan, de Nerval and Oscar Wilde were just a few whose graves I visited.) By seven I'd have returned for dinner.

Of course my feelings would occasionally stage mini riots. I'd become overwhelmed with a longing for Tomaso's body or I'd feel racked with guilt for leaving him or I'd surge with a sudden hatred at how he'd treated me. Once I got so angry my left shoulder swelled up and I had to rush over to Bill's gym for a massage. Mostly I exorcized these feelings by writing long, rambling letters which I didn't mail. Why start things up again? But it was impossible to shut off my mind. Over and over I'd rehearse the most hateful diatribes just in case Tomaso's name surfaced in conversation or I unexpectedly ran into him.

"Tomaso Bianchi? Oh, he's quite a social butterfly alright, though *mosquito* might better describe how he superficially flits over every social scene and gorges himself on whomever he can. He has the light hypnotic buzz of an insect too." Or "Loyalty? Moral integrity? One might do better to choose a public drinking fountain or a urinal for a lover."

I'd never actually say these things but I couldn't stop thinking them. No wonder I got on best with Andrea. She was so intensely present that she'd yank me out of my gloom to look at a worm or play ball. Her delight was infectious.

"Tensho-Roshi says all kids under the age of three are boddhisatvas," Bill said one evening as he, Andrea and I were playing with her blocks.

"Who's Tensho-Roshi and what's a boddhisatva?" I'd been waiting for Bill to give me one of his sermons but had expected something more Christian: sin, redemption and, of course, penance.

"I started doing Zen meditation about a year ago and I really like it," Bill answered simply. "Tensho-Roshi's my teacher, and a boddhisatva . . ."

"You, a Zen Buddhist?" I was flabbergasted. "So you'd now argue that all suffering — shit, all creation — is an illusion? Where does that leave Christ, or me for that matter?"

"Well, it's not quite *that* simple," Bill laughed. "Maybe I'm more a Zen Christian. But you should meet Tensho-Roshi. You might find doing some zazen helpful." Since I was curious and had nothing better to do, I agreed.

The next afternoon we took the Métro to the Gare du Nord, walked to a nondescript brick building nearby

125

and went in. Bill left me in the courtyard and went to find his Roshi. In the corner was a three by five foot rock garden. Two black stones jutted up from a sea of white gravel. The big rocks looked like two whales surfacing or maybe two mountains on a lunar desert. I suppose you can see anything in a rock if you look hard enough. Then I heard a voice behind me.

"Ah, so nice to meet you."

I turned around. An old Japanese man was hobbling towards me with Bill. Sunlight reflected off his shiny bald head and, though his face was wrinkled, his eyes sparkled.

"You come to learn zazen?" My stomach muscles tightened. What was Bill getting me into here? The old Roshi laughed as if he'd read my thoughts.

"But you artist, Bill say. You already practicing then."

The old man laughed again, heartily, as if he'd just told a hilarious joke. Maybe he had. I wasn't sure now if he'd said "then" or "zen."

"What *is* Zen exactly?"

"Exactly? (more laughter) Oh, no big deal. We just sit. But very important, this game, like your art, no? You like some tea? Tea and cookies exactly very yummy."

Something about this laughing Roshi attracted me. I sensed a great power in him yet a teasing slyness that might be troubling were he not so open-hearted. We followed him inside, where he motioned for us to kneel with him around a low table. Then he went through an elegant ritual whipping a fine green powder with a little whisk brush as he poured hot water into our cups.

"This tea very good," he said. "Give flavor of Zen." And it *was* good. Tensho-Roshi's tea had an ambiance more delicious than any I'd ever tasted.


Bill didn't talk about Zen which I found strange considering how he used to go on about Catholic theology. "Just sit," he'd say when I asked a question. "You can only find out by sitting." So I started going with him to Tensho-Roshi's zendo every morning at six.

About twenty people attended. No one spoke. They just removed their shoes, walked to black cushions which were on mats against the walls, and sat down facing the wall.

"What do I do?" I whispered to Bill.

"Just sit with your back straight, hold your hands like this (he showed me the mudra position), keep your eyes half closed, and count your exhalations."

A gong began and ended each session. Occasionally Tensho-Roshi would say a few words afterwards.

"This morning I feel crazy," he began once. "Before I came down to sit with you, I forgot what clothes to put on next. 'Oh, you must put on your *obi*,' I remember finally. That's my belt. Of course, that's a small confusion (he laughs). Usually we have big confusion like how to end suffering. Or should I get married or quit my job. Maybe I go back to Japan.

"So every day we have confusion. This always the condition of our life: either we want, we don't want or we're confused about whether we want something or not. Zen teachers often talk about this, or maybe not. Master Lin Chi shouted at his students, Te Shan hit his, and Huangbo chased his students with stick. I won't do this today because Tensho too old."

(Here everyone laughed. I noticed Tensho Roshi alternated between silly and serious statements, mundane and profound, until one couldn't quite tell which was which.)

"No, today I tell you what is essence of Zen. You like to hear this, no?" Several people nodded. Tensho Roshi laughed again and shook his finger. "But this big mistake. Zen has no essence.

"My own teacher, Daikan Roshi, say we're like glass of water with some dirt in it. If you shake the glass, the water gets cloudy. But if you just let the glass sit, then dirt settles to bottom. Then the water becomes very clear and pure.

"Whenever we want something or say 'This is good' or 'This bad,' judgements cloud our mind. Then we get all stirred up. But when we sit zazen, we're like motionless glass of water. Then we can discover what Buddha call big mind or breath-mind. This is most intimate, pure place for us because it has no intention, no goal. Even to want enlightenment is too much.

"So don't look for anything when you sit. Don't worry is my zazen good or bad. Just sit and watch your breath. Then your practice will be deep and pure. If you can do this, you can take breath-mind into rest of your life. Then you can accept not only your own suffering but suffering of others."

Afterwards, Tensho-Roshi asked if anyone had questions. An older woman said she was finding it hard to sit because her back hurt. "Ah, this very good," the Roshi replied (everyone laughed). "No, I most serious now. When practice difficult, you wake up and concentrate. When zazen too easy you may fall asleep or even get lazy and stop. So our obstacles are very good because they lead us to the marrow of Zen. So you very lucky, yes?"

Next someone asked if it was okay to scratch when they sat. "Scratch what?" Tensho Roshi asked in reply (everyone laughed again). "Let me ask you this," he continued. "What happens if you don't scratch? Pretty soon your itch goes away, yes? Then you've learned something. Our minds so restless; make us itch and hurt. We don't repress these feelings but we needn't invite them into tea either. Itches like feelings and thoughts. At first they seem most strong but if you return to your breath, eventually they pass. Then you've learned something: you're *more* than your itches and thoughts."

For several minutes Tensho-Roshi was silent. He shut his eyes. Finally he said: "Zen like thief breaking into empty house. What can one grab with words anyway? Not much. No eyes, no ears, no nose, no tongue, no body, no mind as *Heart Sutra* tells us. But if you keep sitting zazen, you can begin to penetrate your life very deeply. I say 'your life.' I could say my life, our life, the life of any sentient being. There's no difference really."

Outside in the courtyard a robin chirped. Tensho-Roshi laughed. "See what I mean? Robin say Tensho's lecture finished." Then he thanked us for helping him to practice, got up, bowed to the Buddha on the altar and left.

On most days after zazen, however, the Roshi said nothing. He just smiled as if each moment filled him with infinite amusement. He was like Andrea in this, only his concentration was rock solid. He was also like Andrea in that it was hard to be around him without feeling better.

As I continued sitting, 1 found myself getting calmer. But I was also beginning to feel guilty at living off Eva and Bill. One morning I asked if they knew of any work. Eva said she knew of an art class where I might get a job modeling. I applied and was hired. It was fairly easy, since I was doing zazen a lot and it felt good being around artists again.

One afternoon Eva and I took a stroll through the Luxembourg Gardens where we had our first really long talk since I'd come to stay with them.

ME: I can't say how grateful I that am you and Bill have let me stay with you. I mean you're married now and have Andrea but you've made me feel like family — more than my real family ever did in fact.

(Translation: The words "marriage" and "family" — or rather the politics implicit in these terms — make me feel like an outsider. Kindness only exacerbates this wedge.)

EVA: But you *are* family. You fed me when I first came to Paris. You were my first friend here, and introduced Bill and me.

(Eva reached over and squeezed my hand. Words

divide, touch unites.)

ME: Ya, but then Tomaso and I split for two years. We never even wrote or called. I've been a real jerk.

(Sounds honest but is only a ploy. Actually I'm asking Eva to deny the truth of what I've said and to reinforce my dependance.)

EVA: You're too hard on yourself, Armi. We *like* having you live with us.

(Eva takes the bait. She condescendingly misreads my discomfort as false guilt rather than seeing it as a result of my objective social situation: i.e., my marginalization caused by the reification of marriage which, in turn, generates my low self esteem and egregious behavior.)

ME: You know, I really did miss you. I think I've felt closer to you then anyone except Robbie. With Tomaso there was always this tension. But those early days — remember our first dinner in that Algerian dive? That was terrific. Everything felt possible then.

(I seek to magically leap across our current impasse — which, if pushed further, might land me on the street — by an appeal to nostalgia, a sentimental reconstruction of our past. We chat about the old days for while, then . . .)

EVA: So what do you plan to do with your life now, go back to drawing? I think you should. I was looking through your art notebooks and think you have enough there for a really good gallery show.

(Is Eva hinting it's time I move out? At first I panic, feel resentful. Then I realize she wants to be supportive.)

ME: You think I'm ready for that? Tomaso pulled strings to get me a show in Rome but I don't know if I could swing one here.

EVA: Why not? You have to believe in yourself, Armand. Have you shown your work to anyone who teaches those art classes you're modeling for? I bet they'd help. And if you've already had a show . . ."

We talk on like this for some time. I asked Eva why

she didn't go to Tensho-Roshi's zendo. She had, she said, but taking care of Andrea, keeping house and designing clothes was practice enough for her. "Don't over-idealize that old guy," she said. "He's got hang-ups just like the rest of us, believe me." Before I could ask her what she meant she asked me about Tomaso. Had I heard from him? Was he getting off drugs too?

"What Tomaso does isn't my business anymore," I replied. "Roshi said the other day that too many people want to run after someone or something. It's better to look into oneself."

Eva picked up a leaf off the ground. Clam colored clouds were closing over the sun and the park was getting colder. We began walking back home.

"That's kind of harsh isn't it," Eva continued. "You don't have to be obsessed about someone to care about them. Obsessiveness is selfish but caring — Tensho Roshi certainly cares about people."

"Ya, but he's stronger than I am. He's more detached." For awhile I didn't speak. I was glad we were having this talk but it was beginning to make me grouchy. Obviously there were still some things in myself that I didn't want to look at.

"I care about you," I said finally, slipping my arm around Eva's waist. She slipped her arm around mine. So casual, easy — I felt a warmth of oneness I didn't expect. Had Eva ever been sexually attracted to me I wondered? "I care about Tomaso too, it's just that . . ." I started to feel something I wanted to push back. "It's just that I need more time to sort things out."


December. Three months had passed. Despite occasional bouts of depression, I was starting to feel like the self I wanted to be — or was I simply accepting the self I was? In any event, I was starting to feel good enough to notice others, especially young male others. One kid in the class I modeled for reminded me of myself at nineteen. He had long dark hair and was painfully shy, but I could tell by how he looked at me — with quick, oblique glances — that I turned him on. He was very serious, wore his beret pretentiously at an angle and always took the easel in the back corner by the windows.

I'd have liked to draw him too: the ribbon of velvet shadow that caressed his jaw, his finely chiseled nose, pouting mouth, big limpid eyes, and delicate eyebrows which flowed across his forehead like a stream. When he stepped back to look at a drawing, the muscles of his face momentarily relaxed into the solidity of a hill. I tried to chat with him after class once, but he awkwardly stuffed his drawings into his folder and bounded off. Just as well. Sex was a Pandora's box I feared opening again.

Instead I continued sitting zazen, taking long walks, and reading bedtime stories to Andrea. She'd just hit the age where kids fear monsters, so I drew her a storybook of a monster whose mommy spanks it for running into the street. Andrea liked that. I also followed up Eva's suggestion about contacting a gallery for a show. I was waiting to hear back when I got an unexpected phone call.

"Armand?" The voice on the other end of the line knocked the breath out of me.

"Where are you?"

"In Paris. I thought I was calling Eva. I didn't expect . . . I mean . . ."

My first thrill gave way to a wrenching stomach flip, then a tingling, rising anger. Had Eva told Tomaso I was staying here? He flew up in my mind's eye like a pernicious imp: his teasing eyes, his mocking smile, the salty taste of his neck. Would this horrid spell never break?

"Look, I was just getting ready to go to work."

"I'm sorry. I didn't expect . . ." A long pause. "But since you are, ah . . . well, maybe we could have coffee — if you'd want to, I mean. I'll be here a week. And guess what? I'm c*lean*!" Tomaso in the hospital flashed through my mind, so many tubes protruding from his body that he looked like a shrouded spider.

"Coffee? Well, ya sure. Tomorrow maybe? Give me a call in the morning. I really gotta run now or I'll be late for work." I hung up the phone and dropped onto the couch. All I could hear was my heart pounding in my ears. What audacity for Tomaso to call! (thump, thump.) Why had I agreed to meet him anyway? (thump, thump.) Could I still get out of it?

(thump, THUMP)

I took a deep breath, lit a cigarette, and picked up my journal to page through some gibberish I'd written three months earlier:

> Like blocks of granite stacked precariously atop each other our past actions and refusals to act weight upon us. Like towers of Babel they wait to receive one more block lifted painfully . . . .

Like like like . . . hate hate. My words squiggled about like worms in a frying pan. I didn't need a lover. What I needed was a Pied Piper to drive these obsessive similies into the sea. Or maybe a Buddha to say: "Desires are numberless; I vow to end them." In Buddhist iconography, addiction was pictured as a hungry ghost, an unsatisfied spirit with a tiny mouth and neck, and a huge belly. It wasn't a pretty sight.

The next morning, despite a fitful sleep, I awoke feeling more prepared. When Tomaso phoned about nine-thirty, I suggested the cafe where we'd first met. I didn't want him to know where Bill and Eva's place was because I didn't want him invading my new little haven of safety. Also, I thought I could handle this visit better if

I pretended — at least to myself — that it was our first. In short, I was determined to stay distant, not to let Tomaso pick up where we'd left off. To emphasize this I wore clothes he'd never seen before: baggy pants, a navy blue sweatshirt, red suspenders, a long red muffler, and an old topcoat of Bill's.

Tomaso was already there when I arrived, He jumped up and hugged me but loosened his grip some when I didn't respond. Too late. Already his unique smell (like that of a spaniel) and his irrepressible vivaciousness hooked me.

"Hey, you look great, Armi."

"Ya, I've been modeling. Similar to your work, I guess, except I only pose for poor art students and get just forty francs an hour — not four hundred or four thousand or whatever it is you get. And you?"

"Can't complain. I'm not working but I'm clean. It was your leaving that did it, Armi. Not that OD." Tomaso looked down at his cappuccino cup. Had he just suggested that he still wanted me?

"I'm sorry," I sighed. "I just . . ." I thought a minute. "I couldn't stay detached enough." There, it was out.

"You're clean too, I gather?"

"Ya, ever since I've been here."

Our conversation was stilted. What can two ex-junkies talk about anyway, if not drugs? Neither of us felt like doing that. I felt exceedingly nervous. I mean I was delighted to hear Tomaso was clean — if he really was — and, *if* he was, only time would tell if he'd stay that way. We'd tried too many times for me to believe recovery was a sure bet. What I did know was that I wanted to get out of this damn cafe and walk, where to didn't much matter.

"Say, I've got an idea. Bill introduced me to this old Zen master. Like to meet him?"

"Sure, why not?"

The brisk wind revived me. I realized as we walked up the Rue M. le Prince towards Boul Mich that part of my problem was that I didn't know exactly what I wanted from Tomaso anymore. Maybe he felt the same. So why were we here? Was this walk to be a closure or some new door opening up? In the cold air our condensed breath made wispy, cartoon balloons. I thought of filling mine with a quip of Tensho-Roshi's: "All relationship is illusion and love is crystalized illusion."

Tomaso hunched his shoulders in his black leather jacket and kicked at cans and bits of trash on the sidewalk. Although the day was overcast, he'd slipped on a pair of Cartier sunglasses. A powdery snow was starting to fall, swirling around our legs before shifting about in crazy patterns on the pavement. We were no longer carefree kids hanging out, that was for sure, but we hadn't settled into adulthood either. We paused to listen to a ragged street musician murder a Dylan song. Tomaso smiled as if to say "At least the guy's trying" and tossed a few coins into the kid's open guitar case. Reflected from the cafe window, Tomaso looked like Marlon Brando in *The Wild Ones*. More ravaged, maybe. Who was I then, a burnt out version of the young Montgomery Clift?

We crossed the Seine at the Pont Neuf and headed for Les Halles. I wanted to show Tomaso what remained of our old stomping grounds. The markets had been moved to Rungie, near Orly airport. Now there was only the Bourse with its sixteenth century fluted astrologer's tower and a big hole Parisians called *le trou*, which was destined to become an underground shopping mall. If Les Halles could change this drastically, anything could. Our truly bohemian Paris was dead. Tomaso, Eva and I had been amongst its last revelers. The new Paris was an ugly hodgepodge of vapid boutiques and fast food outlets.

As we walked (until we hopped the Metro for the Gard du Nord that is), Tomaso told me about the drug program he'd gotten into after leaving the hospital. He chattered on about his "steps" and about "turning his

135

life over." It sounded like some kind of weird cult, but I didn't care so long as it worked.

Actually I only half listened, because I was thinking about my dreams of the night before. They were intensely erotic and violent. In one I was fucking Tomaso, when a masked gunman burst in and machine-gunned us. Then the same dream replayed with me as the gunman. A cleaning lady helped us escape down a back stairway, but when Tomaso and I got to the bottom we shot up some heroin. I awoke from that dream sweating, feeling like I was actually loaded.

My last dream was about teaching high school in Brownville again. Don Burton had just fired me, and I walked into the teacher's lounge wondering what to do next. Who should I see there but Tomaso and Robbie. Not only had they been hired to replace me; they were lovers now. Robbie hid giggling behind Tomaso like the little angel with his halo cockeyed. I didn't know whether to feel furious, jealous, or what. To cover my embarrassment I told them about a book I was rereading, Herman Hesse's *Siddhartha*.

"That book's so pompously sentimental," Tomaso said contemptuously.

"Ya, I know. That's why I'm cutting out these quotes which I'm going to rearrange and paste into a new novel." I held up my dogearred copy of the book — all tattered and torn.

"Why didn't you just Xerox the pages," Robbie giggled.

"I've been working on my fourth step," the real Tomaso next to me said. "That's where we make a fearless and searching moral inventory of our lives. Then there's the fifth and sixth step of making amends. That's why I called Eva actually, to apologize for just disappearing on her when we left Paris. So I'm really glad I found you, too. It took your dumping me to make me hit bottom, Armand."

"Hey," I replied, cutting him off. "What's done is

done. We just did what we had to, that's all. Call it karma or whatever. If you need to apologize to make *you* feel better, fine. But don't expect dredging up the past will make *me* feel better. I can hardly deal with the present."

My bluntness surprised me. I'd always tried to please or manipulate Tomaso. If pushed to the wall, I might explode. But here I was saying exactly what I felt without any regard for what his reaction might be.

The Métro jerked to a stop. We got off, silently criss-crossed the honeycomb of tunnels and climbed the stairs to the street. For once, thankfully, no movie posters of Tomaso were plastered on the Metro walls.

"Since we're having this belated heart-to-heart," I continued when we reached the street, "I have a question. Remember our first week in Rome after we left Villefranche?"

"Yes. "

"You said you'd love me forever, remember?"

"Yes."

"Did you really mean that?"

We were now standing at the Rue La Fayette and Rue du Farbourg St. Denis intersection, waiting for the light to change. It was a weird place to be talking like this. The Musée Gustave Moreau would have been better — dark, decadent, lush. Tomaso pursed his lips, stretched, and massaged his lower back before answering.

"Well, I really meant it when I said it, ya."

"Do you still feel that way?"

"I think we still have some deep feelings for each other, ya. Don't you?"

"I guess . . . ."

By now we'd reached the zendo. Someone downstairs told us Tensho Roshi was busy but if we wanted to wait, they'd tell him we were here. I took this opportunity to show Tomaso how to sit and we decided to do zazen together while we waited.

Ever since Tomaso's phone call I'd felt a knot in my

stomach. Maybe it was just anxiety — not knowing what to do. "Our world's a floating world," Tensho-Roshi told me once. "People walk in zigzags, like drunks, and play on the path of life and death. In Zen we discover a third path."

Now that I was sitting, the knot in my stomach became a fist, I kept thinking of Tomaso's answer: "I meant what I said when I said it." Was that all the sincerity or commitment anyone could muster anymore?

Another pain started throbbing in my right shoulder blade. I felt I couldn't take it anymore. I felt I'd have to jump up and scream. Instead, I kept counting my exhalations, tried to breathe out the pain, kept my posture straight and alert. After a while the pain subsided. I could almost see it detach from my solar plexus. It seemed to float out about six inches in front of me and wobble about like a soap bubble. I was sure I could reach out and touch it.

Then I heard the gong. Automatically, as I'd done every morning for the past two months, I bowed to the wall and turned around. I expected to see Tensho-Roshi smiling at us but — except for Tomaso and I —the zendo was empty.

"Who rang that bell?" Tomaso asked.

"It's probably one of Tensho's tricks," I muttered.

We walked back to the waiting room and I asked Tensho Roshi's secretary if he'd come downstairs. "Oh yes," the sandy haired young man said brightly. "He left about twenty minutes ago and said to give you this when you finished sitting." I unfolded the white piece of paper.

"Don't worry," Tensho Roshi's note said. "You'll figure out what to do."

"What's it say?" Tomaso asked.

"Well," I paused, crumpling up the note and stuffing it into my coat pocket. "How'd you like to come back to Bill and Eva's with me? They have a little girl named Andrea now. She's out of this world."

I pushed Tomaso out the front door, massaging his neck and shoulders as I did so. I felt inexplicably freer, lighter, happier than before. Tomaso and I might never get back together but, yes, we did still have deep feelings for each other and that counted for something, surely.

When we got to the corner I looked back. Three schoolboys with bookbags over their shoulders were walking towards us from the other end of the block. One was slugging his friend in the arm. I thought of a poem I'd read long ago: "Beware, dear boys, the bottom of the sea is cruel." Yes, but one had to jump in and learn to swim anyway. What would life be worth otherwise?

Eva was home when we got back, and asked Tomaso to stay for dinner. Since he now had a more receptive audience, I wasn't surprised that the dinner conversation flowed more smoothly than my talk with him had earlier. Nor was I surprised when Tomaso fell into his trademark flirtations. His giggle, for instance. Tonight it neither seduced nor repelled me. I'd long since learned that the more dazzling Tomaso appeared, the more scared and insecure he felt. So I didn't feel left out or jealous. I simply sat quietly, content just to observe and savor their repartee. "Here's this guy I once loved passionately," I remember thinking. "And still do, sorta. But now I'm not so needy, I don't have to put his welfare, or any lover's, above my own anymore." I remember thinking this with an almost palpable pleasure as I chewed on the buttery skin of a baked potato.

What was harder was to refrain from asking Tomaso to sleep over. Half of me really wanted him to, the other half knew better, Not tonight anyway. I was still too shaky, too vulnerable. So while I would have dearly loved to melt against Tomaso's naked flesh again, the very aroma of which could transport me into ecstasy, what I needed most right now was to preserve my boundaries.

What I didn't know was that this was to be the last time I would ever see Tomaso — except in his films, that is. So did I goof up or what? I'd left him (an exhilarating but abusive relationship), he'd found and come after me (if only by accident), and I'd chosen not to let him penetrate the wall I'd built around myself (for self-protection). So why should I have expected that he'd keep trying — pride, stupidity? The faults weren't all on his side, after all.

Tomaso did stay in touch with Eva, however, and I was pleased to hear he stayed off drugs. He also made a few more movies, and Eva wrote to me several months after I'd moved to New York, to say he'd found a new lover, a Swiss kid if I recall. I felt a twinge at that, but had my own art career going now. I'd also discovered gay liberation: lots of sex and partying, no painful entanglements. (Or so it seemed then.) But that's another story. For now it's enough to say this.

When I walked downstairs and hugged Tomaso goodbye that night, I noticed that the snow was falling more heavily. Now it covered the entire street — like frosting on a wedding cake I remember thinking. We'd had some champagne and I was feeling pretty giddy. I was also freezing.

"Well aren't you going to get in the cab?" I asked after we kissed each other hurriedly on each cheek. He did but not until he brushed the hair off my forehead, stroked his hand down my cheek, and clamped it around the back of my neck which he squeezed, a gesture so like Robbie's I felt momentarily addled.

"You taught me how to love, Armi. I hope someday you can forgive me because I really care about you. And I always will, I swear it."

"You're so Italian," I replied, shivering. "But it's been great seeing you. Let's get together again soon, okay?"

We hugged again and Tomaso started to climb into the cab. Then he jumped back, grabbed my face with both hands, and kissed me passionately on the lips. It happened so fast I couldn't resist nor would I have if I'd had the chance. It only lasted an instant — long enough to set my nerves on fire if not my loins — then it was over. Tomaso let go of me, gave me a last piercing glance, ducked back into the taxi, and was gone. I stood watching numbly as he disappeared into the thickening snow.

And what strange snow, too.

In the air the snowflakes swirled whimsically, dancing about as Robbie used to over the hills and fields of the monastery. But once on the ground the snow turned lifeless — as vast and impersonal as eternity. I thought it might have looked blue, purple, even multi-colored reflecting Christmas lights which twinkled from several windows. Instead — illumined by some new kind of street lamp and contrasted against the night — it seemed nothing could add to the snow's whiteness, which was like that of an angel's wing in an icon, a lotus blossom in Antartica, or the face of the one you most love glowing in moonlight, but which later, years later, gets lost in time and space.